MIND MAGIC

THE TRIAD OF MAGIC, BOOK ONE

MACY BLAKE

POPPY DENNISON

For my grandma, who loves me a little bit.
I love you a little bit too.

AUTHOR'S NOTE

Mind Magic was originally published in 2012 under a different name. I have revised and edited that edition and decided to consolidate to a single pen name, so am releasing it as Macy. I hope you all enjoy exploring the Triad of Magic as much as I enjoyed going back and experiencing it again. This series was the first thing I'd ever written, and I never imagined being a published author. It's hard to believe so much has changed in just a few short years.

1

Simon crouched at the edge of the shadow-darkened woods and stared into a clearing where a lone house stood. The knee of his jeans soaked up lingering raindrops from a late-afternoon thunderstorm. The dampness annoyed him, and he quietly repositioned himself so he could wipe away the irritating mud and leaves. He wondered for a moment if jeans had been the best option, then mentally rolled his eyes. It wasn't as if he had a section of his closet specifically for scared-shitless situations. And as much as the wet fabric had served as a momentary distraction, he couldn't deny that he was currently, in fact, scared shitless.

He forced his attention back to the house and looked for any signs of life. Tucked in the mountains of East Tennessee, its rustic yet charming aged-wood exterior and shutter-trimmed windows welcomed visitors and suggested a home where a family lived and loved. A dogwood petal drifted from a nearby tree and landed on Simon's cheek. He blew it off and watched it fall to the ground like a pale-pink snowflake. The cheery blossoms completed the illusion. Their light, sweet scent lingered on the spring breeze as they floated through the air and covered the grass with little dots of color.

This wasn't anyone's happy home, no matter how many dogwoods bloomed merrily in the yard. His magic told him that, called him here over and over, even though he'd been trying for the past two days to ignore it. The dark magic being performed at this place exceeded his skill level, and Simon had never felt anything this evil before.

As an apprentice, Simon shouldn't be handling a situation of this magnitude, but he couldn't keep pretending the screams for help didn't exist. His mage master had warned him time and again to stay away from other magical creatures, to avoid the ones who would take advantage of his power and his very nature.

However, these weren't powerful creatures out to get him. Simon trusted that the very magic that gave him life wouldn't lead him into danger. It must have brought him here because he could help. The voices calling to his mind were children, young ones, and Simon could feel their fear like he could feel his own breath.

The situation was more dangerous because these were not human children. Magical creatures violently protected their young, much like everyone else, but they had additional resources at their disposal. If caught here, it would be a rip-apart-first-and-ask-questions-later scenario. The last thing he wanted was to come face-to-face with a pissed-off werewolf defending its young.

Simon had tried to stay out of it, but two days had passed, and their pack still had not come for them. He had stayed in his house since Friday afternoon, when he'd first heard the calls for help. It went against his nature to ignore anyone who needed him, especially when the very core of his magic told him it was the right thing to do. But helping them went against his training and mage law. Simon didn't think their desperate pleas would penetrate the firmer shields of any better-trained mages, and if they did, Simon was pretty sure the other mages wouldn't bother responding.

They were just children, though, and it was tearing him in two. By Sunday evening, Simon realized he was the only one who would help them. He had to do whatever it took to get those children back to their families where they belonged. Even if it broke all the rules.

Dusk finally fell, and the shadows lengthened to fully darken the clearing. Simon couldn't stand the torment any longer. Five kids calling out to his magic for help was more than he could bear. Now, with the cover of night as added protection, he felt more confident. Simon opened himself to the flow of his magic, and his fortitude increased with the added strength. He might not be as strong as some of the other mages, but the rush of his power opening for him made him believe he had the abilities he needed to get through this unfamiliar situation.

With a deep breath, he lowered his shields and reached out toward the house. He sensed adults there, three of them. Two human and one *Other*. Simon paused at the essence of the third, trying to recognize it without pushing so hard that he gave himself away.

He couldn't identify the murky, clouded mind, so he gently steered his powers away and searched for the signatures of the children. *There*, in a lower level. All five of them, scared and growing weak. Something was draining them of their power slowly and painfully.

One of the humans stepped outside and began walking the perimeter of the house. Dressed in jeans and a camouflage jacket, he carried a hunting rifle. Simon watched him scan the area with military precision, and he feared he'd be found out before he even got started. He shrank back farther into the shadows and used his magic to cloak himself in darkness. The Cimmerian Cloaking spell was one of the first abilities he'd mastered during his training, and it remained one of his strongest talents. Only another mage could see through the spell, and some mages, like the master training him, could hide from others of their kind as well.

Simon used his mind to call the man. He turned and stared at the spot where Simon crouched before he began to move toward him. Simon smiled at the memory of a game he had played as a child and pushed a thought into the man's mind.

Here. Face the tree. Slowly count to a hundred thousand. The man complied and began the count as Simon stepped out of his hiding place. Simon let out a relieved breath that the compulsion had worked and took the gun carefully from the man's hands. He hid it under the low branches of a nearby tree and then crept closer to the house. Looking over his shoulder, he made sure the counting man remained focused on his task, which gave Simon some reassurance he would be safe. He just hoped the spell would hold once he entered the house.

Through the kitchen window, Simon could see the other human standing at the stove, and he heard the man grumbling to himself. "I don't know why I have to handle the damn cooking. Why feed the little shits if he's just gonna drain them dry?" As Simon delved into the man's subconscious, his thoughts became as loud as his mouth. *I wish he would hurry his ass up and finish it so we can get out of here. I don't want trouble with any fucking pack of wolves.*

Yeah, Simon thought, *I wouldn't either.* He sent a gentle nudge to the man's mind: *You must cook all this food for the wolves. They will eat you if you don't cook for them!* Simon covered his mouth to muffle a laugh when a look of horror came over the man's face and he began racing around the kitchen, pulling food from the cabinets.

Who's the little shit now? *Simon thought.*

Finally, there was just the Other left to distract. Humans were easy, susceptible to his suggestions. An Other would probably not be so easy to control, and worse, Simon had no experience to guide him. But the children's fear reinforced his courage, and before he could change his mind, Simon opened the back door and entered the house. The man in the kitchen didn't even look up from his task, and Simon slipped quietly past him.

The Other was down with the young ones, and their distress was growing. The closer Simon got to them, the more their terror grew, from the aching mental thread that had drawn him here to a mind-clenching psychic rope that threatened to strangle his connection to his magic. He fought back his anxiety and followed the cord to the basement door. He opened it, and the smell of their horror made him want to retch into the musty opening leading down the steps into darkness.

Simon placed a hand over his rolling stomach and tried to breathe through his mouth. *It's now or never,* he thought as his nausea eased slightly. He reinforced his cloaking spell, even though he didn't want to use precious energy. Higher-level mages had deeper wells of magic, but it took Simon time to recharge when he used this much power.

Nevertheless, he needed to give himself a little extra time to evaluate what he was up against.

He started down the wooden steps, taking each step slowly to keep the boards from creaking beneath his feet. A single lightbulb lit the basement, but it provided enough light for Simon to see. Shelves of canned goods lined one wall, and piles of dusty boxes took up more of the dank space. From the number of cobwebs decorating everything, the place hadn't been touched in years.

The children huddled together in a corner, where a magical barrier trapped them in place. The sight of their small bodies shivering in the cold infuriated him. Simon didn't know enough about children to guess their ages with any accuracy, but he was pretty sure none of them were over the age of ten. One of them, a boy slightly taller than the others, looked toward the stairs and right at Simon.

He took a protective step in front of the younger ones, and his dark hair fell over his forehead. He tossed it to the side in aggravation and glared at Simon. When he realized Simon wasn't one of their captors, his blue eyes lit up with hope. *A sensitive one,* Simon realized, when the boy saw through his cloaking spell. *Good. That would make this easier.* Simon smiled to reassure him and sent a gentle push into the boy's mind. *I'm here to help. Be ready.*

The boy nodded once and looked away. Simon focused on the Other. Now that he could see it, Simon could gauge its magic. It looked like a regular man, someone you might pass on the street and not give a second glance. A bit skinny, with disheveled light brown hair, the demon would have been unrecognizable if Simon couldn't see the lines of dark magic being dragged from the children and into its body.

Its soul-based magic flowed differently than a mage's, and Simon recognized it as demonic. His apprenticeship had prepared him for the possibility of a demon that looked human, but seeing firsthand a humanlike figure exude such complete dark magic truly terrified Simon. He had absolutely no idea what to do.

With its eyes closed and its head tilted back, the demon revealed the heinous smile on its face as it fed on the magical energies of the

MACY BLAKE & POPPY DENNISON

children. It drained them of their particular brand of magic, as well as their life force, and reveled in every damn minute of it. The demon chuckled, and the kids cried out in pain as dark, jagged lines of magic began flowing from them at a faster rate. The agony of the slow death the demon wrenched from their small bodies suddenly became horrifyingly real.

A savage fury overtook him. Simon concentrated on the spell, its harsh red lines showing just how deadly the damage was to the kids. With a telepathic push fed by his rage, Simon distracted the demon from the spell bleeding the children's energy, and had the creature focus on a conjured enemy by the far wall. He created a monster as repulsive looking as this one made him feel but made sure it was only visible to the demon and himself.

Its bulbous eyes oozed, and its scaly yellow arms reached out for the demon. The demon went wild, letting out a piercing screech that echoed off the dirty walls. It fought and punched at the image only he and Simon could see. The distraction succeeded enough for Simon to move to the enclosure where the children drew together in despair and misery. Their hands covered their ears, and with horrified eyes, they watched the screaming demon. Simon felt guilty for adding to their terror, but he needed the demon occupied so he could work on the holding spell.

Simon began trying to dismantle the strange orange lines of the barrier and felt an immediate drain on his own energy. The magic holding them captive was strong, apparently a talent of the demon's. With a frustrated grunt, Simon focused his power and attempted to unravel it one section at a time. A small opening appeared, and the sensitive boy rushed to it. He began herding the others through until they were all free. Simon let the barrier drop back into place.

To conserve his remaining power, Simon released the cloaking spell he was using on himself. The children jolted in surprise when he appeared. The boy shushed them and looked to Simon for guidance. Simon laid a finger across his lips to remind them to stay quiet and pointed back the way he'd come.

The children made for the stairs, their small bodies making little

8

noise against the rough floor. Simon kept his eyes on the demon and watched it continue to fight its invisible foe. He backed toward the stairs behind them. He'd made it about halfway when the demon broke free from Simon's compulsion and turned to him.

"Mage!"

Simon gathered his strength and sent another mental push, stronger this time. The demon laughed it off and raised its arms, throwing a burst of dark energy that hit Simon in the chest and tossed him back against the stairs. Before Simon could get to his feet, the demon rushed him. It grabbed him by the jacket and flung him away from the stairs. Simon landed against the floor and gasped as his breath was knocked out of him. The demon clambered up the stairs and reached toward where the kids huddled. Simon realized it was conjuring another holding spell; he could see the same orange magical lines forming.

He scrambled to his feet and leapt on the demon's back. It lost its balance and stumbled against the wall. Simon grabbed the rail with one hand and used the other to shove the demon back down the stairs. It hit the floor hard but rolled back to its feet. Simon quickly focused his power and held out his hand to direct his magic. Outside of the cloaking spell, there was only one other at which he excelled: the Torpor Trance. He gathered every ounce of force he could muster and commanded the demon to sleep. The demon stopped moving, its own spell pausing, half-formed. Simon watched in stunned disbelief as it collapsed to the ground.

The children waited for direction at the top of the stairs. A warm trickle dripped down his face as he wearily climbed up to join them. His nose was bleeding, so he pinched his nostrils to stem the flow. His raised arm intensified the ache in his chest where the demon's spell had hit him. Simon tried to access his magic, but only a near-empty reserve remained of his energy. This was getting worse by the moment. He looked to the boy, who returned his gaze with a concerned expression. "I'm fine. Come on. We've got to move fast."

Simon paused to lift the smallest of the children in his arms. Her blonde curls hung damply against her cheeks, and she shivered in his hold. Her T-shirt and shorts didn't provide enough protection during the long hours sitting on the floor. He opened his jacket so he could bring her close against his warmth, then wrapped the sides around her. She sniffled and nuzzled into Simon's neck. "I want my mommy," she whimpered.

"I know you do, sweetie. I'll take you home, okay?"

She nodded and relaxed against him as Simon led them out of the house, past the man in the kitchen, who was still furiously cooking. The cabinet doors stood open and food spilled out onto the counters. The children eyed him suspiciously, and one of the younger boys grabbed Simon's free hand and clenched it tightly.

The group hurried for the woods. The other human still counted where Simon had left him. "Five hundred thirty-seven. Five hundred thirty-eight."

Simon kept moving, ushering the children forward. He glanced back frequently to check on the kids and make sure they weren't being followed. He tripped over a branch and stumbled, but the eldest boy grabbed his arm and steadied him. The children were nearly silent in the woods around him, their shifter magic giving them an advantage in this setting.

He adjusted the little one he held, and she snuggled close to his body heat as her trembling eased. The little boy still holding Simon's hand let out a frustrated huff. "I want to talk to Alpha."

The eldest nodded. "I do too. I thought we could call him when we got away from them."

"Don't worry. We'll be at the car soon, and you can call him once we get away from here." Simon tried to sound reassuring and hoped it helped.

It seemed to work, as the kids all looked at him and nodded. The eldest seemed to realize Simon was struggling in the dark and crossed over to take his arm. The others crowded close and held each other's hands. Simon felt a gentle push against his magic, and it suddenly seemed easier to maneuver in the forest. Puzzled, Simon opened his mind and sensed the body magic in them reaching out to help him. He adapted, his movements smoother and much quieter than before. The kids smiled and seemed much more relaxed.

Simon didn't know how they were doing it, but in a few moments, they were through the woods and to the road where Simon had parked his car. Back on familiar ground, Simon hurried to his little hybrid. He pulled the keys out of his pocket and clicked the key fob to unlock it. The children clambered into the car before Simon even got his door open. The older boy climbed into the front, and the other three scrambled into the back. The brown-haired girl in the back held out her hands for the little one in Simon's arms, and Simon lowered her inside as well. He slipped off his jacket and covered her with it, then got into the driver's seat and started the car.

Simon floored the gas, and the car jerked forward. His eyes flitted back and forth between the road ahead and the rearview mirror. He'd never used compulsions like that before, especially not on an Other, so he couldn't be sure how long the magic would hold. Simon drove on automatic pilot, his course set for town. He pressed one shaking hand to his still-bleeding nose, ignoring his injuries in his eagerness to be as far away from the demon as he could get. Every set of head-lights on the nearly deserted road had him fearing the worst.

He didn't know if the demon would break free of his spell as easily as it had the first one, and Simon wanted to get the kids back to their pack before it could catch them again. Calculating his reserves, he tried to come up with some sort of plan in case their abductors caught up to them. He had little energy left to work with and could only hope to get them home without any further trouble.

Before he knew it, they were back in town, and Simon had no idea where to take the children. He pulled into the parking lot of a small shopping center and laid his head on the steering wheel. Taking a deep breath, Simon focused on gathering his energy and putting his shields back in place. It took much longer than it should have, but after a few moments, he felt steady again and lifted his head.

The children were all watching him closely, their eyes guarded and still suspicious. He turned to the older boy and asked, "Where to?"

The boy didn't answer for a long moment, simply staring at Simon with an expression of curiosity that gave Simon pause. His dark hair had slipped farther down his forehead and into his eyes. Simon brushed it back. The boy grinned and shook his head, forcing the hair back down into his face. It was obviously a familiar gesture. Simon could picture his mother doing the same thing.

The moment seemed to settle whatever question the boy had. He grabbed Simon's hand where it rested on the steering wheel and pressed it to his forehead, then to his mouth and licked it.

Simon felt a burst of magical energy that his empty stores quickly absorbed. He started to pull away, but the boy squeezed his hand, keeping it in his own. He raised his eyes to meet Simon's and bit his lip. He looked puzzled for a moment, as if he were trying to remember something, before he spoke. "I am Garon, son of Gray. I declare you friend of the High Moon Pack."

The other children gasped, and their eyes widened in wonder. They all reached for Simon and gently petted him. The youngest, still wrapped in Simon's jacket, climbed over them all to press a little kiss to Simon's cheek. As they all touched him, their magic began to mingle with his. The ache in Simon's chest eased, and the trickle of blood from his nose slowed to a stop.

Garon smiled a little-boy smile, and a small dimple appeared in his cheek. It seemed to contrast with how calmly he'd handled the situation so far. He released Simon's hand and turned his attention to the road in front of them. "Go toward the old mill. I'll tell you where to turn when we get closer."

The other children settled back into their seats, satisfied with Garon's decision, their wariness of Simon completely gone. Simon rubbed his hand where Garon had licked him and detected a tingle of the powerful body magic inherent to all weres. He would figure it out later, but first, he had to get these children back to their pack.

2

*G*ray pounded his fist against the dash of the SUV, and its driver glanced over at him in concern. "Where the hell are they, Liam?" It was a pointless question, and Gray knew it.

Gray looked over at Liam, his beta and one of his best friends. As kids, they'd often been mistaken for brothers, but now Liam's dark hair and beard contrasted sharply to the gray in his own. The stress lines around Liam's brown eyes showed the tension they both felt. They had driven through and around town, all of their advanced senses on alert for any sign of the cubs who had vanished from their compound two days before. The fact that Gray's own son was among the missing only added to his anxiety, but in reality, all of the cubs were his responsibility.

They stopped in front of an off-the-beaten-track bar, its neon beer signs flashing on and off in an annoying display. "You sure you want to do this?" Liam asked.

Gray stared at the peeling paint on the exterior of Billy's Billiards for a moment, then stepped out of the car. Liam followed, and they entered the bar side by side. The outside may have been dilapidated, but the inside hadn't changed in years. A dark wood bar, polished to a shine, stretched the length of the far wall. The man Gray sought stood behind it.

Several humans sat at the bar, clustered around one end with beers in hand. A television mounted on the wall showed a sporting event in progress, and they all stared at the action like the world would end if they missed a play. Gray and Liam strolled to the opposite end and sat on the wooden stools.

The establishment's owner and namesake made his way down to their end of the bar. When Billy stopped in front of them, he tilted his head slightly to the side, and his gaze flashed down for a moment. Gray acknowledged the sign of respect with a nod. "Alpha Gray," Billy said, his voice low, "what can I get for you?"

"The usual," Gray answered. Billy grunted in acknowledgement of the prearranged signal for information, not alcohol. He turned around to mix Gray's drink. He pulled a glass from the rack, filled it with ice, and poured rum and soda. Someone paying close attention would notice his thumb covered the top of the rum.

When he carried the drink back, he pulled a paper coaster from a stack and placed the drink on it. He glanced down the bar, made sure the humans remained caught up in the game, and nodded at Gray.

"We've got a problem, Bill. Hoping you've heard something," Gray said, his voice so low that only another with supernatural hearing could pick up the sound.

Billy was a lone wolf. Gray's father, former alpha of the High Moon Pack, had given him permission years before to live in their territory without being a member of their pack. In return, Billy kept his eyes and ears open for anything unusual and shared information with them.

As Alpha of the High Moon Pack for the past four years, Gray had only come to him once for anything other than the occasional drink. "Not much going on lately, if you want the truth. It's been quiet."

"We've got five missing cubs, taken by at least two humans and something else we couldn't quite catch the scent of."

"Fuck," Billy whispered. "What would be stupid enough to take werecubs?"

"I don't know. I was hoping you would have something for me to go on. There's more. I can't even mind-speak to them," Gray said. "What could have taken them that could be keeping them from communicating with me?"

Gray had asked himself the same question many times over the past couple of days, and it was another that had no answer. An alpha could communicate mind to mind with members of his pack. It was a little-known fact outside of the were community. Gray had heard nothing but silence from the cubs since their initial cries for help. The fact that something had the cubs, something strong enough to block his connection to them, infuriated Gray. Nothing should be able to come between him and his pack. Nothing.

Billy's eyes narrowed, and a low growl emerged from deep in his chest. "I need to call Mandy. Have her get the kids home. They're with her folks for the weekend."

"Go ahead," Gray told him. Billy rushed from behind the bar and to a door marked "Office." He closed it behind him, and Gray gestured for Liam to follow and listen in, just to be on the safe side.

Gray trusted Billy for the most part, and the other wolf had never given him any reason to doubt his intentions. But right now, he didn't fully trust anyone outside his pack. He considered every member of his pack his family, and everyone else fell into a different category. Gray knew Liam felt the same; he managed the security of the compound and took the duty seriously. Liam stood outside the door, and after a moment, he nodded at Gray to let him know Billy was doing what he'd said.

While he waited on Billy, Gray replayed the kidnapping again in his mind. He desperately searched for some clue, some answer he'd missed in that brief period when all the cubs had screamed for him to help. They'd been at school on the compound when it had happened. The youngest pack members attended a home school of sorts on pack property. The setup kept them away from human children until they were old enough to comprehend the importance of their secret lives.

It was also supposed to provide added protection to them as the most vulnerable pack members. Liam returned to the bar just as Billy

MACY BLAKE & POPPY DENNISON

opened the door and came back over to them. "Mandy's gone to get the kids," he said. "She's bringing them here. Hell, Gray, there's not much out there that can block our mind-speak. It would have to be an Other, probably a mage. They're strong in stuff like that."

"Are there any mages around here?"

"Yeah, there's a few, I think. None that ever come around here, that's for sure." Billy shrugged. "That sort are loners, keep to themselves."

"How can I find them?"

"I don't know," Billy answered. "Never had to find a mage before. There was one that came in here for a while, but he's been dead for ten years or more now. Weird fella. Always smelled like flowers or something. Never caused any trouble, though."

"Any others come in that I should know about?"

"Nah, you know how it is. Everybody keeps to their own kind. Once in a while we'll get a vamp or something passing through, but they catch a whiff of me and head out pretty fast." The humans at the end of the bar signaled for another round, and Billy went to grab more beer from the cooler.

Liam leaned in close to Gray. "This is a bust. Shit, Gray. What do we do now?"

"Call Aunt Maggie and check on Valerie. I'm going to keep my focus on listening for the cubs."

Liam went outside, his cell phone out and ready to make the call.

Valerie was the pack's teacher and taught them the same things any other child would learn in school. The cubs also learned pack history, an important part of their early education. They were allowed to learn, grow, and play as children and wolves, safely on pack grounds. That was the way it was supposed to be, the way it had always been. That day, Gray hadn't heard a word of alarm from her. They'd found Valerie unconscious in the front of the classroom, surrounded by books and papers where she'd fallen.

Liam came back into the bar, shaking his head. Valerie still hadn't regained consciousness. Through the open door, Gray could see darkness had begun to fall. For most, the fading light would have hampered their senses, but it helped their wolves come closer to the surface.

Billy finished serving the humans and came back over to Gray and Liam. "Bill, you heard anyone talking about the pack? Our security measures? Anything like that?"

"Not at all. I'd have called you right away over something like that, Gray."

Gray wanted to punch something. The cubs were provided a guard during class hours as an added precaution. Cade was beating himself up pretty harshly for abandoning his post, even for those few minutes. Emma, the youngest of the kidnapped cubs, had forgotten her lunch. Cade had run up to her family's home in the compound to pick it up. Gone no more than ten minutes, it was long enough for someone to grab the cubs and disappear.

Gray had blamed Cade at first, but after questioning him thoroughly, Gray realized he would have done the same thing. They had always been safe on pack property, and it went against their instincts for a cub to be without lunch when a few minutes' walk up the hill would retrieve it.

The fact that the kidnappers struck when only their teacher was around to protect them troubled Gray. Had they known the teacher was there alone at the time, or had they been prepared to take on a second wolf as well? Gray added that question to the list of those he didn't have an answer for.

"All right, man, thanks for the time and the drink. You let me know if you need anything."

"I will. And say hello to your father for me. How much longer before he can come home?"

"Nine more months," Gray answered. The former alpha was on his required five-year sabbatical after handing over the pack to Gray's control. The rules established by pack tradition were very strict on the matter. Gray's father was only allowed to return to pack grounds for a three-day mourning period in case of the death of a family member. "He won't come unless..." Gray left the thought unfinished.

Billy reached over the bar and clasped Gray's shoulder. "It won't come to that. You need my help, you just let me know, alright?"

"I will. You take care of Mandy and the kids. I'll let you know when we find them."

Gray and Liam went back to the SUV. Liam started the vehicle, then let out a breath. "You sure we shouldn't call your dad home? I don't doubt you, man, you know I don't, but this is some deep shit. We could use the manpower, not to mention your dad's connections with the Council."

"I've already spoken to him, Liam. It's killing him not to be here looking for Garon, but if he does, it puts the entire pack in jeopardy. You know that." If he returned for any reason other than a family death, Gray's position as alpha would be voided, and the pack would be open to any other wolf willing to fight for the right to become the next leader.

Neither Gray nor his father wanted to take that risk. His parents were currently visiting a pack in Oregon, then planned to transfer to a different one in the Midwest. As soon as their five years were up, they could return to Tennessee, with Gray's father taking his place as a Pack Elder.

"I know, Gray. It's just been so long. I'm not giving up hope, but—"

"We'll find them. Any updates from the trackers?" Gray needed to change the subject. He couldn't think of what might be happening to the cubs.

Their best trackers had searched the property. They'd found tread marks from an unknown vehicle on the back road leading out of the compound, and the security cameras installed during Gray's father's reign as alpha were disabled. Three distinct scents discovered nearby belonged to the kidnappers. The unfamiliar scents troubled Gray further. How had strangers gotten into their compound undetected? And how had they known where to find the cubs?

He had no leads, no clues, and no cubs. All he had was his enhanced sense of smell, and he inhaled deeply, the air outside the SUV revealing no trace of the cubs or their attackers.

The majority of the pack searched the surrounding area along with Gray and Liam. The parents of all the missing cubs frantically tried to pick up the familiar scent of their own cubs. The trackers hunted as well, the strange scents they'd picked up from the compound added targets to their search.

Taking a moment, Gray listened again for any sound from the cubs. He focused on Garon, his son, willing their connection into being, but he only heard silence. Some part of Gray knew Garon was still alive, and it was more than just a parent's desperate hope. He could feel the slightest tug of Garon's presence but couldn't trace it.

His thoughts returned to that day. He'd been in town, handling pack business at the local bank when he'd heard the cries for help. Gray had run out of the office, the brief scream of "Dad, help!" running over and over in his mind. The terror in his son's voice would haunt Gray for the rest of his life.

By the time Gray had arrived back at the compound, he'd contacted the rest of the pack, and they had all rushed home from their jobs in town. Everyone present started the search, all of their enhanced senses used in every possible way to bring their children home.

Now sixty hours after the cubs had gone missing, they were still searching. Gray's thoughts were interrupted by his cell phone ringing. After checking the caller ID, Gray answered. "Hey, Becky. No news."

Garon's mother, Becky, currently lived in California with her mate, Alex. When Garon was six, they'd held the celebration to honor Gray's ascension to alpha. She'd met Alex, a visiting wolf from a California pack, and immediately known she'd found her life partner. The discovery had left her with a terrible choice: leaving her six-year-old with his father and following her instincts to join her mate, or staying where she was, without Alex.

Most cubs stayed with their mother in the event of a pack transfer. The heir to the alpha, however, was required to stay with his home pack. Becky's mate was an alpha himself, so there was no chance of him transferring to their pack. She'd denied Alex for nearly a year out of a desire to stay with Garon. In the end, she'd accepted that Garon's place was with his father, and hers was with her mate.

Becky growled in frustration. "Where is he, Gray?"

He wished he had an answer for her. "We're doing everything we can. I will find him, Becky. I swear to you that I will find him."

"He's still alive. I know he is. I can feel him. When my dad passed, it was like this empty place where he'd been, but I don't have that with Garon. Maybe I should come, Gray. I can be on the next plane. Maybe I can find him."

It wasn't a bad idea, and Gray was nearly desperate enough to agree, but Becky's mate wouldn't want her to leave their young cubs behind to go into a dangerous, unknown situation. Gray couldn't blame him for wanting to protect her. "Bec, I won't tell you not to come, but…"

"I know. Alex has gone over and over it with me. I just feel like I should be there, like I should be helping. He's my son, too!"

Gray had never denied Becky access to their son. It was one of the things they'd discussed many times before she'd decided to leave the pack to be with her mate. Alphas typically didn't frequent each other's pack lands, as it was considered a threat to an alpha's territory. The exceptions were only made for pack celebrations. Gray and Alex had worked together to find a way around that tradition so each could be welcomed into the other's pack without any repercussions.

"I know that, and if you feel like you have to come, you know you're welcome here. I just don't know that there is anything you can do. I don't want you here if this gets worse. I swear to you that I'm doing everything I can, using every resource I have. Nothing is more important to me than getting our son back."

"Gray," Becky said, her voice shaking, "do you think this is—"

"No, it's not. You are not being punished, Becky. You did the right thing. Garon is fine. He gets to talk to you all the time, and he gets to see his mother happy. What better gift can you give him?"

It was a discussion they'd had too many times over the past few years. When Gray had come home from college at twenty-three, having attained his BA and master's in finance in five years, he was ready to do nothing but party that first weekend. He'd missed his pack and his friends. One too many beers for both of them had led to a round of sex in the middle of the woods that they'd both regretted afterward, and after a brief period of awkwardness, they'd resumed their friendship like nothing had ever happened.

Until she'd found out she was pregnant. The news had stunned everyone, especially since Gray had made it clear to his pack that although he occasionally enjoyed the company of a woman, he generally preferred men. Add to that fact that unplanned pregnancies were rare in their culture, particularly for an unmated pair. It was expected they'd take each other as mates. But they hadn't, and the uproar it had caused still made Gray angry.

After a while, everything had settled down, and they'd raised their son like any other couple living apart, splitting time and sharing responsibilities. When Becky had met Alex, it had turned her world upside down. She'd realized before any of them what accepting Alex as her mate would mean and had turned him down flat. She would not leave her son, and that was the only option available.

When Becky had made the choice to go to Alex, she'd convinced herself she would be punished for her actions, no matter how many times they all tried to reassure her that she was being ridiculous.

Nearly sobbing, Becky said, "Gray, promise me you'll find him. I just need to hear it one more time. I know you will, but please, just say it once more."

Before Gray could answer, he felt the tug of excitement from Cade, then a call through their mind-link. *Alpha, the cubs have returned. They are safe.*

"Becky, they've been found. He's safe. I'm on my way back to the compound. I'll call you back."

He heard her burst into tears of relief as he hung up the phone. *I'm on my way, Cade.*

3

Simon followed Garon's directions to a gravel road that was barely visible due to the large trees surrounding it. The spring leaves from the oaks created a canopy that blocked out what little light the night sky provided. About a hundred feet in, Simon could see a tall fence that ran in both directions, and the road was blocked by a large black gate.

His headlights only allowed him to see so far, so Simon stopped in front of the gate and looked to Garon for further direction. The boy pushed the button to lower his window and made a low yipping sound. A moment later, a lower yip was returned, and a man stepped out of the woods with a large, almost black wolf at his side. Having never been this close to a werewolf, it shocked Simon how big these men could become in animal form.

The humans seemed just as big, as evidenced by the man who now approached Simon's car. Dressed all in black, his bald head reflected what little light could be found. He rested his hand on the holstered weapon at his side, and Simon had no doubt he would draw and fire before Simon even realized he'd moved. Needless to say, Simon stayed very still.

The man approached Garon's side of the car and leaned in to sniff and rub against the boy. He reached in and petted the other children for a moment as well. Movement on his side of the car drew Simon's attention. The wolf had come around to stare at him through the side window. Its breath fogged up the glass slightly with each exhale. With a gulp, Simon jerked his eyes back to the front.

Garon reached over and patted Simon's arm, and Simon jumped. The boy grinned and turned back to the man at his window. "We need to see Alpha, Cade."

"I've already called to him," Cade replied. "He's out searching. You okay?"

Garon nodded and turned back to Simon. Garon smiled and tried to reassure him. "It'll be okay. You don't have to be worried."

Simon glanced over at the wolf staring in his window, then back to the boy. "Easy for you to say."

Garon barked out a little laugh and turned back to Cade. The man rested his hand on Garon's shoulder, squeezed slightly with his fingers, and rubbed a little path back and forth with his thumb. Cade's hand seemed so large against the boy's shoulder, reminding Simon again how young these kids were.

He could feel the excited energy building in them and wondered why they weren't all jumping out of the car. They all seemed to know they had to stay where they were. Even the little one sat contentedly in the backseat, curled up against one of the other kids. She smiled now, her little cheeks revealing dimples that had Simon giving her a quick grin in return from the rearview mirror.

Staring ahead again, Simon began to pick out the shapes of other wolves on the darkened side of the gate. Now that his eyes were adjusting, he saw they were all huge and would be eye to eye with him where he sat in the car. None of them looked pleased. Simon's fight-or-flight instinct was going crazy, with every fiber of his being screaming at him to get the hell out of there and away from all the weres.

Just when Simon thought he would crack from the tension, Garon turned and looked out the back window. A black SUV appeared and slid to a stop inches from Simon's bumper, its headlights lighting up the interior of the car in a sudden burst of brightness. A large man stepped out of the passenger's side and came toward the car. As big as the bald guy with the gun, the new man's hair was almost totally gray. Even his mustache and beard were gray. And so was his shirt.

Before he could take the time to wonder over the odd color choice, Simon could feel the strength of the gray guy's presence, even without opening his magic to see him more clearly. His power was so forceful it made Simon's breath hitch, and he leaned back in his seat, trying to keep from having a panic attack and embarrassing himself.

All the kids yipped happily and bounced around. They'd been waiting for this man. It really didn't surprise Simon at all. Anyone that powerful had to be in charge. Simon's theory was confirmed when the man nodded, and Cade opened the back door. The kids piled out and surrounded the man. He dropped to one knee, petting them all and, Simon noticed, sniffing them. This man was the alpha of the pack, a term Simon had only read about.

Garon opened his door and stepped out. The alpha met his eyes, and Garon grinned and ran the few steps to him. The alpha stood, scooped Garon up against him, and held him tight. They rubbed their faces together for several long moments. The alpha's eyes met Simon's through the window. Simon could read the distrust and anger there, but also a touch of gratitude. Simon's panic settled a notch. He might make it out of this yet.

Although the alpha still held Garon tight against him, the boy turned his head and unwrapped one arm from the man's neck. He beckoned to Simon, and Simon reluctantly opened his door and climbed out of the car.

The wolf at his window stalked immediately to his side. It intimidated the hell out of Simon, especially as he drew closer to the alpha and saw how huge the man was. Simon was not exactly short at five foot ten, but this guy seemed to tower over him. As he forced himself closer, Simon realized the alpha wasn't actually that much bigger—only three or four inches at most—but his substantial presence made him seem like a giant.

Simon felt a tickle in his mind. Garon was trying to communicate with him through their link. Tearing his focus away from the alpha wolf was a challenge, but Simon opened himself up and heard the boy. *What is your name?* Garon asked.

He'd never gotten around to introducing himself. *Simon,* he answered.

Garon nodded and turned back to the alpha. *Holy shit,* Simon thought, *he's the alpha's son.* The light from the cars illuminated the area enough that Simon could see their eyes were the same clear shade of blue, and although Garon's dark brown hair contrasted sharply against the alpha's gray, the resemblance between them was unmistakable.

Garon met the alpha's eyes again. "Dad? Can you put me down now?" His voice held the slightest tone of exasperation, and Simon forced himself not to smile. Safely home by his father's side, Garon received a reassuring hug and rebounded into a growing boy who didn't want to be babied.

The alpha reluctantly lowered his son to the ground and took a moment to brush Garon's hair out of his eyes before settling his hand on his son's neck to keep him close. When he leaned into his father's strong legs, Garon's actions belied his earlier bravado. "Dad, this is Simon, friend of the High Moon Pack."

Simon noticed the tightening of the alpha's body at Garon's declaration, and tensed, but no one made a move toward him. Everyone waited to see the alpha's reaction. He looked Simon up and down in a frankly assessing manner. Simon wondered if he imagined the heat in the stare, but his body reacted anyway. Blood began to pool in places he would rather it didn't when surrounded by an angry pack of wolves.

The alpha reached some sort of conclusion and stepped forward, his son by his side. "Welcome, Simon, friend of the High Moon Pack. I am Gray, Alpha of the High Moon Pack. Thank you for returning my son and our cubs."

Unsure of the protocol in the situation, Simon recognized the formality of the speech and bowed his head slightly. "You're welcome?"

Simon wasn't quite able to keep the question out of his voice. His knees shook a bit from anxiety, and his heart pounded double time in his chest. It didn't help that the alpha took one step closer to him. He gave Simon a second look, and this time Simon had no doubt the alpha was checking him out. It sparked something inside him that he didn't need to be thinking about.

Garon and the other cubs snickered and drew Gray's attention to them. They quieted immediately, but the distraction allowed Simon to get his thoughts back on track. His cheeks heated with embarrassment, but he fought the impulse to keep his eyes lowered. As powerful as Gray was, he wasn't Simon's alpha. Simon knew better than to appear too submissive, even if his overactive hormones wanted him to roll over and beg.

Gray gestured to the combination of men and wolves surrounding him. "Take the cubs to the meeting hall. Gather everyone together. Liam, with me."

Everyone rushed to do as their alpha commanded, and the cubs were piled into the SUV Gray had arrived in. Big, bald Cade turned to lift the little one, but she slipped away and ran back to Simon. The wolf who had intimidated Simon earlier stepped in her way, but she darted around him and lifted her arms to Simon. He picked her up, keeping one eye on the wolf standing beside him.

"Thank you," she whispered, then snuggled her face into his neck.

Simon hugged her gently, then set her back on the ground. As she ran back to the SUV, he realized she still had his jacket wrapped around her. It made him smile. She could have it; he had an old one in the back of his closet.

When everyone was through the gate, Gray returned his attention to Simon. They locked eyes for a long moment, and Simon's knees went wobbly again. The intensity of his stare, his sheer potency, drew Simon under his spell. The moment seemed to stretch on and on before the alpha finally spoke. "Explain to me how you have our missing cubs."

His voice was softer now, which surprised Simon. He'd expected more of that anger, perhaps a threat or two, or at the very least a strongly worded demand for answers. There was none of that in Gray's words or even in his tone. Just the softest statement, his eyes locked on Simon's.

Unsure of how much he should actually reveal, Simon tried to find some reasonable explanation. He couldn't. What would these wolves do to him if they knew a mage stood right here in front of them? As if that wasn't bad enough, the desire he felt to throw himself at the alpha sent his thoughts scattering, while warning signals tap-danced up and down his spine.

Gray took a step closer. Simon fought to keep his breathing under control. "Simon, my son has made you a friend of our pack. This means that we cannot harm you. You are under our protection."

Simon's eyes widened, and he stepped back. "How did you...?"

"I can smell your fear. Now tell me what I want to know."

Feeling the hole he'd dug for himself get deeper, Simon let out a frustrated breath and began. "I am Simon Osbourne, Apprentice Mage of the Earthhavens." Watching Gray's eyes widen, Simon rushed on. "I know I'm not supposed to get involved with you guys, but I could hear them in my head, calling for help. What was I supposed to do? I knew they were kids, cubs, whatever you call them, and no one else was coming. I couldn't just leave them there to die! So I went there and found them and got them out and brought them home. That's it. I swear it."

Gray's eyes darkened, and Simon didn't know what the new expression meant. "Who took my son, Simon? Who had our cubs?"

Oh God, that look. The illusion of gentleness became the stare of an alpha determined to get what he wanted. Simon replied, "A demon and two human men. The demon drained them of their energy somehow." At the word demon, the wolf at Gray's side began to growl, and Simon took another step back. "I'll tell you where they are, but please, you have to let me go. I'm going to be in so much trouble as it is."

Gray stepped forward and reached toward Simon. Simon flinched but relaxed when he felt Gray's hand on his face, gently wiping below his nose. "Were you injured?"

The blood from his nose created a deep-red streak on Gray's

thumb. Simon shook his head. "No, I'm okay. Just drained a bit. Can I go?"

"Yes, Simon, you can go. Just as soon as you tell me where to find them."

Simon gave Gray detailed directions back to the house.

4

The majority of the pack volunteered to go with Gray on the search mission. They all wanted a piece of whatever had taken the cubs. Gray chose a group of ten of his strongest and fastest wolves to take to the country house. They parked their vehicles by the road, and half of them shifted into wolf form. The rest armed themselves with weapons and headed into the woods.

Gray remained in human form, a loaded handgun in his right hand. The left he shifted so his nails turned into sharp, thick claws. Liam and Cade flanked him in wolf form. Even though Gray didn't like it and wanted them to all stay focused on the hunt, his beta and best friend were duty-bound to protect him as well.

Everyone slowed as they drew closer to the house through the woods. They could hear a voice. Gray held up his hand, signaling for everyone to stop moving. "Seven thousand, three hundred sixty-four. Seven thousand, three hundred sixty-five."

What the fuck is that? Cade's voice asked Gray through mind-speak.

Gray shrugged and motioned for them to start moving again.

"Seven thousand, three hundred sixty-six."

Two wolves approached the human on either side. They growled low and deep, fangs bared and hackles raised. He didn't acknowledge them.

"Seven thousand, three hundred sixty-seven."

Gray approached, his weapon primed and ready. "Don't move," he said, his gun leveled at the man's head.

"Seven thousand, three hundred sixty-eight."

That's fucking annoying, *Liam grumbled.*

Gray agreed. *Take him down.* The other two pack members attacked, one wolf hitting the human in the chest, the other using his body to swipe the man's legs out from under him. Within seconds, he was pinned with a wolf muzzle around his neck and another ready to strike his abdomen.

"Seven thousand, three hundred sixty-nine."

"Shut him the hell up."

"Gladly." A pack member still in human form pulled a roll of duct tape from his bag and ripped off a strip. He covered the human's mouth with it and pressed down harder than he needed to, but it did muffle his voice. Another wide strip of tape secured the human to the tree.

"The mage said two humans and a demon. Be on your guard." Gray started forward again. The wolves preceded him, and all their senses were on high alert. They surrounded the house and circled around until they met up again at the back.

Another human in the kitchen, Cade said. Any sign of the demon?

A round of negative answers came through the link. Gray's shoulders tensed in aggravation as he sent the word out to the team. *No one saw the demon.*

Move in? Liam asked.

Gray nodded. He stayed back with Liam and Cade while two of their pack members kicked open the door. Three wolves rushed into the kitchen and tackled the human standing at the stove. He tried to crawl away, but their combined weight on top of him kept him from getting very far.

"No, no, no!" he screamed. "I cooked for you so you don't have to eat me!"

Food covered the counters, and each burner on the stove held a pot with something bubbling away inside it. Jeff sniffed at one of the pots on the stove, wrinkled his nose, and took a step back. "The mage must have done it," he said. "I heard they could do parlor tricks like this."

"Focus," Gray commanded. "Forget the fucking food and secure him. Find the demon."

The human continued to beg as they taped him up until his mouth was finally covered. They began searching the house, and Gray's frustration grew as each room turned up empty. It took precious time, but they secured the house before they went down to where the cubs and Simon said they'd left the demon.

As soon as they opened the basement door, Gray began to lose control, his wolf demanding to be set free.

The room reeked of the cubs' fear. He wanted vengeance. His wolf wanted to rip something to shreds. He stormed back up the stairs and grabbed the human in the kitchen by the throat.

Gray slammed him against the wall. His fangs extended, and his voice dropped to a low, deep growl. "The Other, the one from the basement. Where is it?" The human tried to answer through the tape. Gray ripped it off with one vicious pull. "Answer me."

"He left. He didn't want to eat. I don't know where. But you can have it. It's all for you. I'm almost done now. Almost done! Please!"

Gray tossed him aside and his body landed against the cabinets with a thud. "This is pointless. What the fuck is wrong with them?"

The pack members had all gathered in the kitchen. One of them spoke up. "It was the mage. He did it, I bet. Some creepy shit if you ask me."

Several of them nodded their agreement. "Do you think he could do this to us? Control us like this?"

Gray didn't know, which angered him further.

"Why didn't he just kill them?"

"I don't know," Gray growled. "We need to focus on finding the demon. Back outside, everyone, and stick together. It can't have gotten far. We'll worry about the mage and his magic later."

The demon, however, was nowhere to be found. They searched the house and the surrounding area but found nothing except its lingering scent. They recognized the smell as one they'd picked up after the kidnapping but couldn't follow it for long. It grew fainter before simply vanishing.

Members of the Pack High Council arrived to take custody of the humans, who would be questioned and dealt with according to pack law. As much as Gray wanted to deal with them personally, a situation of this magnitude, one that broke all known tradition of keeping to themselves, had to be handled by someone who knew more than he did about the Others.

More questions needed to be answered, and the Council left questioning Simon to him, for the time being. They decided not to force Simon to remove his compulsions. They wanted to take the opportunity to study the spells he used to see what they could learn about his abilities. The members of the Council weren't the only ones who wanted to know more about Simon. The mysterious mage had lingered in Gray's thoughts since the moment he'd driven away in his tiny green car.

Gray hadn't taken the time to process the attraction he'd felt for Simon, that simmering heat that came out of nowhere the first time he'd laid eyes on the mage. Oddly, the cubs were all enamored with him as well and praised his bravery during their rescue. Even Garon, who typically disliked strangers, made sure Gray knew Simon was "awesome." His son had also let him know Simon had been hurt in the process, more than he'd let on. Garon's description of the demon rushing Simon, Simon getting hit with a spell or something so strong that it had knocked him off his feet, and then doing whatever he'd done to get the demon to drop where it stood, had been told with such wonder that Gray began to feel a bit of awe for the mage himself.

And now he had Garon's amazing mage as a friend of the pack, and a pack that was a bit freaked out over what said mage had done to the humans. When you added in the lust Gray felt for Simon, the intensity like nothing he'd ever felt before, the hits just kept on coming.

Nevertheless, his son and the other cubs were safely home, and Gray was determined to keep it that way. The combination of fear and fury that had kept him going for the past few days eased into a simmering rage. Unanswered questions never sat well with him, especially when it came to his pack's safety.

After a few hours spent dealing with the repercussions, Gray stood in the doorway of his son's bedroom and watched Garon sleeping peacefully in his own bed. Garon twisted around beneath his blanket, and his hair fell into his face again. Gray walked quietly over to the bed and brushed it back. Garon let out a soft breath and snuggled into his pillow.

Gray dropped to his knees beside the bed, exhausted from the past few days. He needed to rest but couldn't bear to leave Garon alone just yet. He leaned his head onto the mattress and reached up to slide his hand under Garon's. His son's fingers closed over his, and Gray began to calm, the stress and fear fading as he drifted to sleep.

After a few hours' rest, he woke up feeling calmer and more in control. He quietly closed the door to Garon's room and followed his nose to the kitchen to let Aunt Maggie know he'd be leaving. As suspected, he found her standing at the stove, making their breakfast. Gray swiped a piece of bacon and avoided the spatula she swung at his hand. He completed their morning ritual by placing a quick kiss on her head.

"Morning, Alpha," she said.

Gray's father's oldest sister had the same gray hair and blue eyes that all the members of their father's line possessed. Her hair was twisted up into a knot on the back of her head. Combined with the apron she wore over her clothes, she looked a bit like a grandmother from a Norman Rockwell painting. Of course, if Gray ever mentioned that to her, she'd swing more than a spatula at him.

"Morning, Aunt. I need to head out on some pack business. You'll be okay with Garon for a while?"

She turned from the stove and gave him the look only mothers can give. Her children might all be older than Gray and out on their own now, but she still had the look down perfectly. "Do I need to tell you to be careful, nephew?"

"No, ma'am."

"Good. 'Cause I can see the rage in you, boy, and don't think I can't. There's a reason why we don't mix with the mages, and happenings like this are one of them."

"I understand. I have to get some answers, though. This pack depends on me for their safety, and I won't let them down."

"No, you won't. There's untapped strength in you that you'll be needing soon enough. Your father trusted you to lead this pack, and he was right to turn it over when he did. Clear your mind and trust your instincts. And if you ask me one more time if I'll be okay watching that boy of yours, I'll show you just how well I can use this spatula as a weapon."

She surprised a smile out of him. Gray knew he didn't need to ask; Aunt Maggie had helped him with Garon from the beginning and had stepped up to help full time when Becky had left. As she'd told him then, she was bored and needed something to do besides sit around and knit socks. Gray didn't know what he'd do without her.

"No need to get violent." He grinned and backed away slowly. She huffed at him as he left to find the mage who had won his son's trust so quickly and completely.

IT WAS easy enough to track Simon down. Liam had had the presence of mind to memorize Simon's license plate number, and then all they needed was some quick maneuvering on the computer. Gray left the hows up to the more technically inclined members of the pack and focused on the results.

Gray would have missed the turn if his GPS hadn't told him he'd arrived at his destination. The driveway was much like the one onto the pack lands, surrounded by trees and tucked into the landscape. The similarities ended there, however. Simon's home didn't have a huge fence or a gate covering the drive. Carefully organized flowers and shrubs lined the path, and as Gray continued down the drive, he admired the time that must be spent maintaining so much land-scaping.

The little cabin was also encircled with flowers, and Gray was left to wonder about this mage who appeared so different from every-thing he'd been taught in the past. The mages he'd heard of were dark and dangerous men, quick to kill anything that threatened them or stood in their way. They didn't live in an idyllic country cabin surrounded by beauty. And they didn't rescue werecubs who had been kidnapped.

Simon was clearly different, and as Gray stepped from his truck, his interest in the mage grew. This was not his enemy, but Simon wasn't his friend. Yet. The thought gave him pause. Why would he even think about befriending a mage? His father wouldn't, Gray knew that, but his father wasn't here, and Aunt Maggie had always told him to trust his instincts. His instincts were telling him to keep Simon close, closer than he'd even considered before this very moment.

Before Gray reached the door, he heard a groan of frustration from the backyard and the quiet sounds of Simon mumbling to himself. Gray followed the sound of Simon's voice, not quite able to pick up the words even with his enhanced hearing.

Rounding the back of the house, Gray found Simon sitting cross-legged on the grass. The sun turned the bare skin of his chest a golden brown and highlighted his chestnut-brown hair with a multitude of colors, from blond to the darkest of reds.

Simon looked a bit older in the morning light, closer to his midtwenties than Gray had first thought. He was slim, probably a little too thin for his size. Aunt Maggie would want to feed him a pound of bacon a day to put some meat on his bones.

Gray could feel the tingle of magic in the air, fluctuating wildly as Simon chanted quietly to himself. The power faded, and Simon slapped the grass at his side. Gray cleared his throat, and Simon's head jerked up in surprise. He scrambled to his feet, revealing long legs barely covered by the shortest red running shorts Gray had ever seen. Gray took in the view of long, lean muscles and attempted to curb his suddenly overactive hormones. This wasn't the time to imagine those legs wrapped tightly around his waist.

"Alpha Gray, what are you doing here?"

He forced his eyes up to Simon's face. "Hello, Simon. You can just call me Gray."

Simon dropped his gaze to the ground. "Gray." A burst of arousal scented the air. Gray's hormones weren't the only ones playing havoc.

He stepped forward and raised Simon's chin with his fingers. The urge to lean in and take a quick taste of Simon's full lips consumed Gray. He leaned forward a bit before catching himself and taking a step back. Simon licked his lips, and Gray followed the motion of Simon's tongue with his eyes.

"I..." Gray paused to clear his throat when his voice sounded huskier than he intended. "I have some questions about yesterday, if you have a few minutes."

"Oh, well, hmm... of course. Sure."

The sweet smell of desire twisted into the sour tang of fear. Gray growled in annoyance. If nothing else, he didn't want this man afraid of him. "I won't hurt you, Simon. I just need some answers."

"I know," Simon said, "but it really isn't a good idea for you to be here. This is really frowned upon. I am going to be in so much trouble."

"I'm not here to cause trouble. I just need to understand what happened to our cubs, and you're the only mage I know."

Simon took a deep breath, visibly trying to calm himself. "I'm told there are good reasons for that." The smell of fear faded, which pleased Gray more than he wanted to admit. "I'm not sure how well I can answer, but ask your questions, and I'll tell you what I can."

"Thank you. What do you know about the demon who had the cubs? It was gone by the time we got there, and we weren't able to track it."

Taking a moment, Simon seemed to think over what he'd been able to gain from his confrontation with the demon. "It was odd. At first, I thought the power I read signaled a low-level demon, but it broke free of my mind magic surprisingly fast."

"Why is that weird? Aren't all demons strong in magic?"

Simon's brow furrowed, and he shook his head in surprise. "You really don't know about this, do you?"

When Gray shook his head, Simon explained further. "Think of magic like a triangle. At the top point is mind magic. That's what mages use. The next point is body magic, like you and the other were-creatures have. The final point is soul magic, which is usually what demons are strongest in. Make sense?"

It did, but Gray really didn't think what he could do was magic. "I've never really described what werewolves can do as some sort of body magic. We just are what we are," Gray said.

"That's true for most cases. A mage is a mage, and that means he's strongest in mind magic. But then there's someone like Garon—"

"Garon? What about him?"

"Well, Garon is sensitive to mind magic. He communicated with me mind to mind. But he must be able to do body magic as well, correct?"

"Do you mean can he shift? Yeah, he can shift. Only at the full moon, though. He's not old enough yet to control the change at will."

"Hmm, I've never considered that. My course of study hasn't involved very much information on were-culture. I really haven't had the opportunity to study anything outside of the mage's realm of influence."

Gray ran his fingers through his hair, wondering just how far he should push this. He needed to learn more about magic, especially if his son could do it. "And Garon can do this magic of the mages?"

"Some of it, yes. I don't know how much, but I know he mind-talked to me with the ease of another mage."

That didn't really surprise Gray very much. "He's used to that, Simon. I can talk mind to mind with the members of my pack."

It was Simon's turn to look surprised. "You can? But that's mind magic!"

Gray shrugged. "All alphas can communicate directly with their packs. It's always been that way. This demon did mind magic as well, but that really isn't as unusual as you made it sound if we can do it too."

"You're right. This isn't the way it was explained to me at all." Simon paced around the small yard, shaking his head. "None of the books mention any of this, not that I've seen anyway."

Gray wondered what else Simon's books failed to mention, and how he was going to get the information he needed to not only protect his pack but to also help his son.

5

*S*imon forced himself to stand still and face Gray. He didn't know what it was about this man that sent his thoughts flying in a thousand different directions, but he found it incredibly hard to focus with Gray's clear blue eyes watching every movement.

He pulled his bottom lip between his teeth while he thought and watched as Gray's eyes dropped to his mouth. Simon's breath caught in his chest, and he licked his lips again. Gray's tongue mimicked the action. A little trail of dampness glistened on Gray's lips in the bright sunlight. *Focus,* he told himself. *This is not the time for flirting.*

Simon broke his gaze from Gray and crossed the yard to his patch of herbs. He plucked a sprig of lemongrass from its overflowing terra-cotta pot and stuck it between his teeth. The tangy citrus flavor helped him regain control of himself.

"Are you eating grass?" Gray asked.

The horrified look on his face made Simon laugh. "Well, in a way. Here, try some." He pulled another piece from the plant and handed it to Gray.

Gray eyed it curiously before putting it in his mouth. "That's... odd. Smells familiar, though."

"It's lemongrass." Simon shrugged and felt himself start to blush. "It helps keep me calm."

Gray worked the blade of grass between his teeth for a moment before taking it back out. "It doesn't taste bad."

"Nope. It makes good tea. And Thai food. Um, if you like that kind of thing."

"I do."

"Good." Simon laughed. "This is ridiculous. I wish I wasn't so nervous around you."

"You don't have any reason to be, Simon."

"But that's the thing. I do. You have to know that our circles stay separated for a reason. If I'm caught spending time with you, I will most likely lose my apprenticeship."

Gray tossed his lemongrass aside and stepped closer. "I don't want to get you in trouble, but you have to know that I need answers. That thing took my son, our cubs."

"I understand, and I'm going to try my best to help. Maybe I could just call you?" Gray stared at him again so intently that Simon's stomach fluttered.

"We can start there." Gray pulled his cell phone from the front pocket of his jeans. "Number?"

Simon recited the digits and ran inside for a piece of paper and a pen. When he returned, Gray jotted his number down and handed the pad back to him.

"I'll try to find something in my books. I don't know what's going on, and I can't exactly ask anyone without getting in trouble."

"Just do your best."

"I will."

Gray reached up and brushed his thumb over Simon's lower lip. "You take care of yourself, Simon. Call if you need anything."

Simon watched him leave and let out a long breath. He went inside for a cold drink and sat at the kitchen table with a few of his books. His concentration had been scattered since he had first heard the frightened werecubs in his mind days before. Now he had another source of distraction in the form of a large alpha werewolf determined to get the answers he needed.

Problem was, Simon wasn't sure he was the mage for the job. He clearly wasn't as educated as he liked to believe, no matter that he'd spent hours poring through the books his master provided him. He had other resources, the books his grandfather had collected over his years of study, and they were all just steps away inside his cabin.

Technically, it was against the rules for him to study them without his master's permission, and Simon knew he'd never receive it. Until he reached full mage status, his studies were focused on what he needed to progress. These were special circumstances, though. Weren't they?

Especially when the circumstances involved an alpha werewolf who evoked such a strong physical response in him. Even Simon recognized the flaw in that argument, but when Gray had looked at him earlier, the heat in his gaze had burned all the way to Simon's toes.

He pushed the books aside in frustration. He'd looked through them already and knew they wouldn't help. Instead, he went back outside and attempted to center his energies for the third time that day. He focused on his backyard garden, felt the cool grass beneath him prickling at his bare legs, and let his mind concentrate on the sensation. He opened his other senses and smelled the flowers and herbs growing beside him, picking out the soothing scents of daffodil and rosemary, the strange combination one that Simon was sure only he found comforting. He meditated on the natural elements and drew power toward him.

Centering himself should be second nature at this point in his training, and Simon was determined to master the skill. Most of his peers were well on their way to becoming masters by the time they were his age, but Simon couldn't even get past his apprenticeship, and his twenty-fifth birthday was only weeks away.

Simon could feel the gathering energy slipping as his negative thoughts grew. He tried to force those thoughts back into a box in the far corner of his mind. He pulled out his favorite memory, that of watching his elderly grandfather sit in this very spot and the look of peace on his face as he drew power from the earth.

The memory worked, and Simon's focus returned for a brief moment, until his thoughts wandered to the heated stares he'd shared with Gray. He considered the fact that Gray was older, had a child, and was probably very happily mated to Garon's mother. That didn't stop him from wanting to explore his feelings, but it would stop him from acting on his attraction. His mind kept drifting to what he'd rather be doing during their forbidden time together. The fact that it had more to do with the carnal than the educational helped him stand his ground.

He would call Gray and tell him he hadn't found out anything. That would be the end of it, Simon was sure. As tempting as it was to allow himself to take a quick look at his grandfather's books, it would be the wrong thing to do. Master Thomas allowed him to keep the collection in his residence only after receiving a strongly worded promise from Simon that he wouldn't use them until he'd been approved to do so.

As if sensing Simon's wavering allegiance, Master Thomas himself appeared around the corner of the house.

"Good afternoon, Simon!" Master Thomas was always cheerful when he first arrived. His cheer wouldn't likely last, since Simon had not only failed to center himself properly, but also had a rather large confession to make.

Simon bowed slightly, giving Master Thomas the respect he commanded. In his early thirties, Thomas wasn't that much older than Simon. Simon was actually his first apprentice. When he had first met Thomas five years ago, Simon had been immediately attracted to the man who would be training him.

Knowing they'd be spending the majority of their time alone together hadn't helped much at all. Thomas was Simon's height and slim, as most mages tended to be. He kept his bright blond hair immaculately styled, and his perfectly straight white teeth always showed when he smiled. Simon was strangely attracted to those perfect teeth. It had always puzzled him.

His thoughts wandering again, Simon considered that perhaps he needed to look up one of those online sites his friends back in community college had told him about. Problem was, Simon wasn't big on casual hookups, and that was really all he could manage right now. Although, perhaps if there was a site like HotGayMages.com, he would be able to have his cake and eat it too.

Forcing his ideas for online research into the back of his mind, Simon greeted Thomas and took his outstretched hand. He watched as the bright white smile fell from his master's face.

"Simon, what is the explanation for this? You clearly haven't progressed since our last meeting. I'm extremely disappointed."

"My apologies, Master, I've been…" Simon paused, trying to find a way to explain his actions. "Distracted."

Thomas let out another of his long-suffering sighs, the ones Simon had nearly grown immune to over the past few years of his training. "This is something you should have mastered in your first year, Simon. Come, let's perform the training bond so you can center yourself and we can get to work."

Simon tried to control his flinch, but Master Thomas saw it and scowled.

"Sorry, Master. You know how painful I find the training bond."

Thomas's frown deepened. "You've made that clear. However, I know of no other way to get you focused so we can accomplish the tasks I have set for us today." Thomas led the way to the back of the garden, where Simon's grandfather had created a circle of special plants that enhanced the connection between two mages. It was Simon's least favorite place in his entire yard.

They sat together in the circle and joined hands. Thomas's grip was familiar, his hands slightly larger than Simon's, and his skin smooth where Simon's was work-roughened from his time spent gardening. Simon took a deep breath and relaxed, then opened his shields to allow his master to reach the magic inside him.

Thomas's magic was older, stronger, and overwhelmed Simon's own as soon as it entered him. It was a shock, the abruptness of the change in power, and Simon had to fight to maintain his open state and allow the centering to occur.

It seemed to take longer each time they had to do this. When Simon's energy began to respond, Thomas jerked away, and it left Simon shaky and unbalanced.

"Simon? What is this I sense in your magic? There is Other there where there was none before. Explain yourself immediately." Thomas's voice was harsher than Simon had ever heard it.

Simon took a breath and struggled to retain his control as his anxiety levels spiked. He had so hoped Thomas would not be able to sense his activities. He should have known better. Most days, it seemed his mage master understood Simon's magic better than Simon did.

"There was an incident this weekend involving some werecubs and a low-level demon," Simon explained. "I know it goes against our code to become involved with other magical creatures, but they were just kids, and they needed help. I really felt that it was the right thing to do." Simon braced himself for the reaction he knew was coming.

Thomas's mouth tightened into a line, and his eyes burned in anger. "I clearly don't need to tell you in how many ways you went against our code with your actions. There will be consequences for this, and I fear they may be dire ones." At that, he dropped Simon's hands and shook his head sadly. "However, that decision is not up to me. I'm afraid I will have to take this directly to the Conclave. I am extremely disappointed in you, Simon. Your actions reflect poorly on both of us."

Simon cringed at Thomas's words, having never considered that his involvement with the weres would negatively impact his master's status. "My apologies, Master, for not recognizing the effect this situation would have on you. It was never my intent to cast any sort of shadow on your abilities."

"This is the core of your problem. You must consider your actions more carefully. You must focus. You are so close to reaching your goals, but no matter how hard we try, you never seem to cross that line. I hesitate to push you harder, but I am afraid that I must, and now we have these repercussions from the Conclave to consider. We are running out of time. In a couple weeks, I will no longer be able to guide you."

It was the first time Simon had heard this news, and it shocked him. "What does that mean?"

"You know what it means, Simon. If you have not progressed by your twenty-fifth birthday, I will have to report to the Conclave that you are unable to achieve mage status. At that time, I will be assigned a new apprentice, and you will not be allowed to study and advance within our group. I'm sorry, Simon, but you must see that you can no longer allow yourself to be distracted by trivialities. Time is of the essence, and your progression as a mage must be your first, and only, priority."

Simon hadn't known, actually, and the thought of never being able to become a mage in full devastated him. It had been his dream since childhood, when his grandfather had first recognized the gift in Simon. His grandfather had managed Simon's education in his early years, until his death when Simon was thirteen.

Simon had become even more set on his path after he'd lost his grandfather. It was his way of honoring his grandfather's memory and one of the reasons he'd accepted the cabin as a bequest when he turned eighteen. The cabin and a generous sum of money had been held in trust for him until that time. His grandmother knew it was meant to be Simon's as he followed the path her husband had so many years ago.

"It's my only priority, Master Thomas. I'll prove it to you." Simon forced his mind away from everything else, determined to become a mage and fulfill both his and his grandfather's dream. If the occasional stray thought of bright blue eyes and steely gray hair invaded his mind in the future, Simon would tuck them away as a curiosity that was better forgotten.

6

"That is not acceptable," Gray said into the phone Thursday morning. "I need that system updated ASAP. What do I need to do to make that happen?"

One of Gray's first priorities after the kidnapping was to upgrade the compound's security system. The disabled camera on the back gate was only the beginning of the changes. A new guard schedule had been created, with a majority of his pack members volunteering more of their time to take on additional shifts.

For the more technical side, Gray had used a contact of Garon's stepfather, Alex. He knew a were from another pack who specialized in security. The upgrade was going to put a large dent in the pack accounts, but for Gray, there was no question that there needed to be some serious changes made to the way they protected themselves.

Rocky "Don't Make Fun of My Name" Harris explained the problems he encountered due to the rushed request. "There's really nothing else I can do, Alpha Gray. You wanted the best, and that's what I'm getting for you. Unfortunately, some of the components I need for your system are on backorder for another week."

"And then we're looking at another week to get everything here and installed?"

"I know you're frustrated, and so am I. I could do a substitute, but honestly, it's not worth it. We're only looking at a few days' difference either way you look at it."

Gray pounded his fist against the desk. Every day his pack went with less than adequate protection was another day they were more vulnerable to a second attack. "Just do what you have to do, Rocky. Pay for overnight shipping, put pressure on them, whatever it takes."

"Already done and I'll do it again. These guys want to keep my business and want me to be happy. They'll jump through a few hoops for me if they can to get it done earlier."

"I appreciate it."

"No problem. Did you get the new guard rotation worked out like I recommended?"

"It's done—a bit hard to decipher, but we've got it in place."

"Excellent," Rocky said. "Imagine if it's hard to figure out for you guys, how hard it will be for anyone trying to find a weakness in the routine."

"Good point."

"I also wanted to let you know that I've cleared my schedule for next week. If it's okay with you, I'd like to fly out personally and handle the installation."

"It's more than okay with me. Alex trusts you completely, and I know he wouldn't have recommended you if you weren't the best."

"Alex is a good friend. I wish all alphas were like you guys. Anyway, I'll be there as soon as I finish the job I'm on. I'll let you know the details in a couple days."

They finished their call, and Gray hung up the phone. The issues with the compound's security were just one of many he'd been dealing with this week. The humans they'd captured, who were working with the demon, had been questioned by the High Council.

The Council member who had called with the results was highly amused. Apparently, they hadn't been able to get anything out of the first human until he'd counted to one hundred thousand. Once he'd reached that magic number, he stopped and looked around, wondering where the hell he was.

The second was too scared he was going to be eaten and would only talk when he was in the kitchen, cooking. They had never seen anything like it before and wanted to know more about the mage who had planted such entertaining suggestions in their minds.

It wasn't quite the reaction Gray had expected, but he had to admit he was just as fascinated by Simon. He couldn't get the mage out of his mind, his thoughts circling back to Simon frequently since he'd seen him last on Monday. Gray found himself in the unusual position of regretting his promise to stay away. He wasn't a man who frequently had regrets.

As tempting as it was to call Simon and ask if he'd learned anything new, Gray forced himself to focus on the tasks at hand. He was frustrated by his lack of knowledge surrounding other magical beings, and although Simon would be an excellent resource, he needed to get information from other sources as well.

He was an educated man, and over his years of study, he'd done more research papers and dug through more obscure references than he cared to admit. Even his current role managing the pack's finances required a large amount of analysis. But all that experience didn't help him one bit when trying to learn more about the world in which he currently found himself entrenched.

Every child of the High Moon Pack received training in their ways from an early age. Pack history, rules, and traditions were all emphasized from the beginning of a cub's education, in addition to how to deal with living in a human-dominated world. However, study of the other creatures that coexisted with them had never been part of that schooling. Mages, demons, vampires, and all the rest were just Other, and not important to them.

That being the case, Gray had few resources at his disposal. He'd discussed his concerns with the Council, and they'd assured him that they were going to do everything they could to help.

Aunt Maggie entered his office, dust rag in one hand and a bottle of furniture polish in the other. After nearly five years of trying, Gray had given up the fight with her over cleaning the house. She didn't

MACY BLAKE & POPPY DENNISON

acknowledge his presence, just started removing items from the shelves.

The office was pretty much as his father had left it. Very traditional in style, the walls were lined with dark cherry bookcases, and the desk was a large antique table that matched. Gray had replaced the worn-out upholstered chairs his father had added years before with two overstuffed burgundy leather ones.

Photographs of Garon filled the few empty places around the room. Aunt Maggie lingered over one of him, dressed only in a diaper, laughing and playing outside in the sprinkler. After a moment, she carefully wiped it off and put it back in place.

"I'm worried about Garon," she said.

Gray was as well, but he waited for her to finish her thoughts. Aunt Maggie liked to talk things out and often needed a quiet listener while she worked through a problem.

"He's not himself since he came home. I expected some of that, as I'm sure you did. I'm not saying you haven't been great with him, because you have, it's just that he seems so disconnected somehow." She stopped and looked at him, waiting for a response.

"I agree. I haven't been able to speak to him through our mind-link since he's returned. Garon told me that the demon did something when they were taken, some spell, and that he's not been able to talk to me since then." Gray tried to stay positive, but he couldn't quite keep the undercurrent of worry from his voice. He'd taken for granted the ability to communicate with his son through their link, to hear that comforting hum of Garon's presence in his mind. He'd thought at first Garon was somehow shutting him out, but then he realized there was nothing but silence from all the kidnapped cubs. "I'm hoping that as his wolf gets stronger, he'll get back to himself."

"I'm sure you're right. It's probably because he's recovering. I just need to give him time. Are the other kids doing okay?"

"Little Emma has been doing well. I spoke to her father yesterday, and other than wanting to sleep with them at night, she seems to be doing fine. I felt her connection strengthen yesterday and hope she's

MIND MAGIC

able to communicate with me today. I'm sure Garon and the others will get better too."

She nodded, her worry soothed a bit by his reassurance. "That Emma is such a cute little thing."

"She sure is. The rest are doing as well as can be expected. None of them have reconnected with me yet, but they are all growing stronger. They're all staying close to home and their parents right now," Gray said.

Maggie turned back to the bookcase, removed a few books, and laid them carefully on the shelf below. After spraying the empty space with furniture polish, she wiped it down, then stopped and stared. Gray heard her sniffle and looked up to see her shoulders softly shaking. He quickly stood, moved behind her, and wrapped his arms around her shoulders. He hugged her gently as she cried.

"This is all too much, Gray. I don't understand why this happened. It doesn't make any sense at all."

"No, it doesn't. I'll figure it out and keep us safe."

She seemed to need his reassurance and wiped her eyes before shrugging off his hug. "Of course you will. Now, what are we going to do about Garon?"

That was a very good question and another on Gray's list he didn't have an answer to. Garon was in that strange age between little boy and teen, when he didn't want to be babied but wasn't mature enough to be treated more like an adult. Gray missed the days when Garon would crawl up on his lap and chatter about his day, telling *Daddy* his secrets and adventures.

"We'll take it one day at a time and keep a close eye on him. That's really all we can do." Gray could only hope he wasn't wrong.

THAT evening, Gray and Garon were in the kitchen making dinner. Garon liked helping, especially when they had burgers and fries, his favorite meal. "Kiddo, can you grab me the Worcestershire sauce and an egg from the fridge?"

53

"On it!" Garon ran over to the refrigerator and rattled the bottles in the door as he jerked it open.

"Easy!" Gray laughed, enjoying his son's antics.

"Sorry, Dad." Garon grabbed an egg from the carrier and then snagged the bottle of sauce from the door. "Nothing broken." He slammed the door and made everything rattle again.

He handed the items over with a sheepish grin and resumed watching Gray add his "secret ingredients" to the meat. "Hey, why's it called Worst-a-cheer sauce, anyway?"

"Worcestershire," Gray corrected, "and I don't know. Probably because that's where it's made." Gray added a splash to the meat then handed the bottle back to Garon.

Taking a sniff of it, Garon turned up his nose. "It's kind of stinky if you ask me. What's in it, anyway?"

"I'm not sure. Check out the label. It'll tell us."

Garon read while Gray cracked the egg open and added it to the mixture. "Gross! Dad, it has anchovies in it!"

"Gross," Gray agreed. "But it sure does taste good in burgers."

"Yeah. It's kinda weird how there's so much stuff in it, don't you think?" Garon put the lid back on and put the bottle away. He opened the door with comic slowness and closed it in the same way with a smirky grin.

Gray laughed as Garon came back over to the counter. "You can be silly all you want, but that door is going to fall off one of these days, and you're going to clean up the mess!"

Garon snorted. "Nope, I've learned my lesson." He waited for Gray to finish adding salt and pepper to the bowl of meat, then took a deep breath and asked, "So, mixing up all this stuff together in the burgers makes them taste better, right?"

His son's face was very serious, after he'd just been laughing the moment before. Gray tried to figure out where Garon was going with this line of questioning but had no idea. He decided to just go with the flow, hoping Garon would reveal what was on his mind. "Well, I think so. You want to mash them up?"

It was Garon's job to mix the meat and press it into patties. They switched spots, and Garon stuck his hands into the mess. "So, some-times, mixing things up is okay, right?"

"Well, I suppose so. Depends on what you're mixing up."

"Yeah. This meat is cold, Dad."

"Want me to take over?"

"Nope, I can do it." Garon continued mixing, his face set in concentration. "Dad, can I ask you something important?"

"Of course."

"Why did that demon thing hurt me?"

"I'm not sure, kiddo. But I've got tons of people working with me trying to figure it out."

"I know. It's just… well, I think I'm kind of mixed-up now too."

Giving Garon a little nudge with his arm, Gray asked, "But not with anchovies?"

Garon laughed and wiggled his meat-covered fingers at Gray. "Eww, anchovy guts!"

Gray dutifully made a disgusted face and then laughed. After grab-bing the potatoes from the bag in the pantry, Gray dumped a few in the sink for their fries. "You know, I feel kind of mixed-up sometimes. I could try to help, if you want to talk about it."

Garon nodded but didn't say anything else. He finished making the patties and waited until Gray finished cleaning the potatoes to wash his hands in the sink. Gray continued working on the potatoes, chop-ping and seasoning them before putting them in the oven. "Ready to grill?"

"Yes!" Garon went out the back door to their deck and waited while Gray loaded the burgers onto the preheated racks. When he was done and the lid was closed, they sat down on the patio chairs. "Dad?"

"Yeah?"

"I think that demon guy did something to mix me up." Garon's voice broke a little, and he turned his head away and wiped his hand over his eyes. "I mean, I can't hear you anymore, and you can't hear me either. I kinda feel sick too. Like, my stomach kinda hurts, but I'm not going to throw up or anything, and my head hurts, and I'm pretty tired. Do you think the other kids feel bad like me? I mean, everybody has just stayed home this week, and I haven't gotten to play with my friends like I always do. I don't know if they're okay or anything."

Gray stood up and went over to Garon's chair. "Oh, kiddo, I'm sorry you've been worried about them. I didn't think about that. We just wanted to keep everyone home for a few days, you know? But we can call and check on them after dinner if you want."

"Yeah. We probably should, just to be sure."

"No problem. We'll call after we eat, and how about we call Granddaddy and Mimi also. Granddaddy told me he was going to do some reading on all this stuff."

"Cool. I miss them. I wish they could come home."

"Me too. Not much longer now, though. What, nine more months or something?" Gray knew Garon was counting down the days, a game he played with Gray's parents when they called.

"Yeah. Granddaddy said they'd be here for Christmas this year." Garon looked slyly over to Gray and smiled. "He said he was going to get me a new Xbox."

Gray pretended to be shocked. "What? No way! Xbox is crap. PlayStations only allowed in this house."

Garon laughed, just as Gray knew he would. "Yeah right, Dad. PlayStations are for old people. You know, like you."

They both cracked up, and Gray went to flip the burgers. "When we go in, I think you should take some medicine for that belly ache and headache you've got." Garon hated taking medicine, even when it tasted like candy. He'd always complained that it tasted funny and had spit it out, even as a baby.

"Gross, Dad. I'd rather eat anchovy guts."

7

*S*imon rubbed slow circles on his aching stomach while holding a damp cloth over his eyes. A mug of cooling chamomile tea sat on his bedside table, a book of herbal home remedies open beside it. Nothing he'd tried seemed to help, and Simon considered making a trip to the clinic in town to see if he had the flu or something. His magic had never made him feel bad before, but maybe something was wrong there. He hadn't been feeling quite right since the demon had attacked him.

He couldn't remember ever feeling this unwell. His grandmother used to tease him that he had inherited his grandfather's healthy constitution. Every fall he battled hay fever, and he took St. John's Wort daily to help his stress levels, but other than that, he didn't get sick. Headaches, stomachaches, general weakness, and being tired weren't exactly life-threatening symptoms, but the fact that none of his treatments had helped for nearly a week concerned Simon.

It was times like these when Simon wished he had a man in his life. It would be nice to have someone to make him a fresh pot of tea and to run the damp cloth over his eyes through some water to cool it down. Heck, just someone to snuggle up next to him and rub his hair would be nice.

With a groan, Simon pushed his patchwork quilt aside and struggled his way out of bed. He snagged his too-cool tea from the nightstand and went into the kitchen for a new mug. He wondered if he should call Master Thomas and ask for help. Simon acknowledged he'd been pushing himself very hard magically over the past few days, determined to prove his ability to become a full mage. From sunup to sundown, he worked on his magic. He kept himself centered and accomplished most of the tasks Master Thomas had left for him after their disastrous visit earlier in the week.

Waiting for the kettle to boil seemed to take an eternity. He was hungry but couldn't really convince himself to eat. The thought of even a saltine cracker made his stomach roll. He nibbled on one anyway, hoping it would help a little.

The kettle whistled and Simon poured the hot water over a diffuser of his herbal tea mixture. While it steeped, he wondered if Master Thomas had heard back from the Conclave of Mages. His actions would have been reported by now, but since he'd never been in any kind of trouble before, magical or otherwise, he wasn't sure exactly what the process was.

With a quiet sigh, he dumped the used tea leaves into the trash and went back to bed. He sipped his tea and read through his book, thankful when the chamomile started doing its job, relaxing his tense belly and easing some of the nausea. Maybe all he needed was a good night's sleep.

Sometime later, Simon sat up quickly in bed and looked around the room. Nothing seemed out of place, and he didn't hear any noises. He blinked away the remnants of sleep and focused on his surroundings. Something was wrong. He could feel it.

His body ached when he stood up and pulled on his robe. His thin flannel pajama pants and T-shirt didn't protect him from the chill in the night air. The cold wood floors against his bare feet made Simon wish for a pair of warm slippers. He made a quick pass through the cabin but didn't find anything unusual.

It must have been a dream. He paused at the thermostat and considered turning the heat on but resisted the urge. It would warm up later, and he would regret the wasted energy. Simon went back to his bedroom, the need for sleep pulling desperately at his tired body. Before he could settle back beneath the covers, he felt a slight pull against his magic. It made his head ache even more, and he pressed a hand to his forehead to combat the pain.

He opened his magic just a little, the throb in his head more intense at that small use. Simon could sense someone hovering at the edge of his awareness. All he could feel was fear and pain. His thoughts immediately turned to the cubs. He whispered *Hello* in his mind and jerked in surprise when a weak and quiet answer came through.

Simon? Is that you?

It took a moment for Simon to recognize the voice as Garon's. *Garon? It's me, Simon. What's wrong?*

I don't feel very good, and I can't wake up, and my dad can't hear me. Can you help me?

I have your dad's cell phone number. Let me call him, okay?

Okay. Simon, will you stay with me?

No problem, big guy. Just let me grab my phone.

Simon stumbled into his office and unplugged his phone from its charger. He scrolled through his contacts until he found Gray's listing and hit Send. As the phone rang, he sent comforting thoughts through to Garon.

Gray's voice was muffled and low when he answered. "Hello."

"Gray, it's Simon."

"Simon? It's two in the morning."

"I know. Sorry to wake you, but I need for you to go check on Garon."

Simon heard the rustle of quickly moved bed covers. "What's wrong?"

"I don't know. He called to me mentally and is scared."

Simon could hear Gray's footsteps and then a door opening. "Garon?" There wasn't a response. "Garon. Wake up, son." Still no response. "Simon, he's not waking up. What's going on?"

"I'm not sure. Let me see if I can talk to him again. Hold on."

Simon focused his mind back on Garon. *Garon? Your dad is there with you. Can you tell me what you are feeling?*

Garon's voice was very weak when he answered. I don't know. Just bad. And I can't wake up. Simon, can you come over?

With only the slightest pause, Simon answered, *I'm on my way.*

I'm really scared. Will you tell my dad to stay with me?

Of course. He's not going to leave you. I promise. Let me talk to your dad again for a second, okay? Just hang on, and I'll be there to help.

Simon refocused on the phone at his ear. "Gray, Garon is asking me to come and help him. I told him I would." While he talked, Simon grabbed his car keys from the hall table and shoved his feet into his bright yellow Crocs.

"You can help?" Gray asked.

"I don't know. But I'm going to try."

"I'll call the gate and let them know to let you in."

"See you in a few. Call me if there are any changes."

"I will." Gray hung up the phone as Simon started his car.

It seemed to take forever for Simon to get to the pack's compound. He drove as fast as he could. He talked to Garon through their mind-link, the only way he knew to comfort the scared little boy. By the time he arrived, his anxiety was at an all-time high and threatened to overwhelm him. He tried to keep his fear hidden from Garon.

The gate opened the moment he arrived. Two guards waited for him. The big bald guy—*Cade*, Simon thought—came to the passenger door and tried to open it. Simon's doors locked automatically, and he fumbled with the switch to get them open.

When the lock clicked, Cade pulled the door open and got into the car. "Go," he commanded.

So Simon went down the dark road into the compound. It required his total concentration, the headlights barely lighting the path in front of him. They reached a T in the road.

"Left," Cade directed. Simon turned left.

Cabins lined the path, tucked back into the woods. Simon barely noticed them, keeping his eyes on the drive. The narrow road made him nervous, and he tried to keep from slipping off the edge of the graveled area. "Stop here," Cade said.

Simon's brain took an extra moment to relay the message to his foot, and the car came to a stuttering stop. He parked in the middle of the road, but before he could ask where he should go, Cade jumped out of the car and came around to Simon's side. He moved fast and had opened Simon's door before Simon could even gather his thoughts. Simon blinked at him a moment, his head and stomach aching fiercely and his thoughts racing.

Cade reached in, grabbed Simon's arm, and pulled him out of the car onto the pavement. Simon stumbled, his body not accepting his commands. *I'm here, Garon,* he whispered through the link. *I'll be right beside you in a moment.*

He didn't get a reply.

Cade led him into a large house, but Simon couldn't even focus enough to take in his surroundings. He knew there were stairs and remembered climbing them and Cade's arm steadying him as they went.

Gray stood in front of a door. Simon felt a slight ease in his aching body in the alpha's presence. It came right back the moment he stepped into the room and saw Garon's small body curled up on his twin bed.

The blankets were dark blue, nearly black in the darkness of the room. As Simon got closer, he could make out little stars and planets decorating them. "Can you turn on a light?" he whispered. Gray turned on the little lamp on Garon's bedside table.

Simon's eyes were drawn to Garon's face, his pale cheek resting against a yellow circle that must be the sun. He ran his hand over Garon's forehead and felt the unsettling coolness of his skin. Simon knelt beside him and brushed Garon's hair back. With a deep breath to fortify himself, he opened his magic.

He cried out in pain. Something was there, inside the boy. Some-thing magical, and it drained Garon of any magic he held. Simon couldn't grasp more than that through his own agony. Something was hurting Garon.

He heard a frantic voice behind him, Gray's words loud in the otherwise quiet room. "Simon, what is it?"

Simon shook his head, waving Gray away. This couldn't wait for explanations. Garon didn't have enough time for that. Whatever this thing was, it had to be stopped before it killed Garon.

He heard Gray's voice again in the background. "Call Aunt Maggie. Get her here. Call the other parents. Have them check the rest of the kids."

Oh God, Simon thought, *the others*. He couldn't worry about them now. They weren't here. Garon was. He had to fix this before he could do anything for the rest of them.

Simon concentrated and tried to get a feel for the magic. *There.* He could just see the little lines of current sucking power away from Garon's magical core. A dark spell, different from anything Simon had ever seen before, stole the life from this little boy, eating away at him from the center of his being.

A nebulous void, it surged and sparked with each passing second as it fed on Garon's life force. Simon felt the moment the parasite became aware of him, of his magic. He sensed it reaching out to him, trying to attach itself to him in its hungry quest for more, but it couldn't breach his shields and turned back to finish draining the little energy left in the boy. The light around Garon's small body faded, the dim glow of his aura barely visible.

Simon tried to deflect the lines using a simple distraction spell. Nothing. He tried to unweave the magic, move them outside of Garon and away from his core. Nothing. He created a bubble around it. Nothing worked. He banged his hand on the bed in frustration.

In a panic, Simon opened himself wider and dropped his shields completely, something he had never done outside the security of his own home. He did the only thing he could think of and grabbed hold of the thing that leeched the life out of Garon. With every bit of power his magic possessed, he yanked at that dark void and ripped it away from the dying boy.

He felt himself falling, the thud of the carpeted floor against his back, and then the slam as the spell that attacked Garon turned on him. Simon couldn't stop it. With his magical barriers down, he was unable to keep the leech out of his body.

The dark magic began to attack Simon's core, and his body started shaking. He wouldn't be able to hold it off for long, but he had to if he hoped to help Garon survive. He rolled over to his knees and saw movement out of the corner of his eye. One set of feet passed him, but the other remained in his vision. A warm hand pressed on the center of his back. He flinched away from the touch, afraid the magic would try to find yet another victim before he could contain it. He crawled his way back to the bed.

It wasn't going to get another piece of this boy, but Garon wouldn't make it if he didn't have some help. While he wrapped that nasty leech tight into himself, Simon divided his magic, willed it into two pieces. One trapped the dark spell inside him. When he had it contained, he clenched Garon's hand in his and fed the rest of his magic to Garon. He heard the springs creak on the bed and heard muffled voices, like shouting underwater. *Gray, calling frantically to his son*, he reasoned.

Simon watched Garon's body buck, heard more angry shouts behind him. Garon's eyes fluttered open and locked on Simon's.

"Simon, no!" Garon's voice surprised them all. Gray and Cade responded instantly to the strength of his plea. *Too late*, Simon thought. He smiled at Garon and felt himself being jerked away. He landed on the floor, Cade's hand on his chest, holding him down. He turned his head toward the bed and watched Gray grab his son, saw their arms wrapping tightly around each other.

Garon spoke, but Simon couldn't seem to make out the words. He was okay, though. Nothing else mattered. Both sets of clear blue eyes turned to him.

Simon tried to smile again, but it didn't work. He met Gray's stare and acknowledged the gratitude in them. It was enough. He closed his eyes.

8

*G*ray watched in frustration as Simon's eyes drifted closed. He didn't know which way to turn. He held his son, his awake and alert son, in his arms. Simon wasn't so lucky.

Simon's body lay where it fell on the floor of Garon's bedroom. His ridiculous green-plaid pajamas and bright orange T-shirt twisted to expose his stomach. One bright yellow shoe sat on the floor next to his bare foot.

Garon squeezed Gray with his arms to get his attention. "Dad, we have to help him."

Gray knew that, wanted to help, but didn't know what to do. Cade lifted his hand from Simon's limp body on the floor and stared down at the unconscious man. He'd no doubt thought Simon was hurting Garon and had jerked the mage away from his alpha-heir. Cade looked up at his alpha for direction. Gray couldn't tell him anything. He'd never felt so helpless.

Garon struggled out of Gray's arms and went to kneel at Simon's side. "He gave it all to me, Dad."

"All of what?"

"His magic. I could feel it. I didn't have any left, and then he saved me."

Hell. This was worse than he'd thought. Gray really had no clue when it came to magical stuff and hadn't had a chance to learn much with everything else going on.

"Okay. Well, we'll just have to figure out a way to fix this."

"I should give it back."

Gray stopped himself from shouting his answer. "No, Garon. Simon gave you his magic for a reason." He moved to the floor and knelt on the other side of Simon's still form. "Now we have to figure out what was going on so we can help him. Right?"

Garon nodded. "You're right." He paused, his eyebrows scrunching together before they relaxed and he smiled. "You'll just have to give him some of yours."

Cade jumped in before Gray could respond. "No way."

A low growl filled the room. Cade's eyes widened, and he looked at Gray. It wasn't coming from Gray, though. It came from Garon.

He snarled at Cade, his face beginning the shift, which shouldn't have been possible.

"Garon, stop!" Gray's deep and commanding tone allowed for no disobedience. It was the first time Gray had needed to use his alpha voice on his son.

Garon immediately complied, lowering his eyes and baring his neck to his father. He took several deep breaths then looked back up at Gray with tears in his eyes. "He doesn't get to tell us what to do."

"Garon Nathaniel Townsend, you will not disrespect an elder member of this pack at any time. Do I make myself clear?"

"Yes," Garon grumbled.

"You're right that Cade doesn't tell *me* what to do. However, he is one of my trusted friends and advisors, and you need to learn to listen to those you trust. Understood?"

"Yes," Garon said again, this time wiping angrily at the tears in his eyes.

"Now, as *you* are also one of the people I trust, tell me why you think I can give Simon some of my magic."

His son's head jerked up in surprise, and he had a happy smile on his face. "Well, since Simon gave me all his magic, it's only right that we replace it, Dad. I mean, when he got hurt after that demon thing hit him with that spell, the other kids and I helped him get better."

Gray absorbed that little detail for the first time and fought back a scowl. "And how did you do that?"

Garon tilted his head to the side. "What do you mean? We just did it. Like if one of us got hurt and we helped them shift to wolf form to heal. Like that."

Like that. It seemed easy when Garon explained it, but it altered Gray's thinking completely. Cade's as well, apparently. "But Garon, your dad calls our wolf. Simon doesn't have a wolf."

Garon rolled his eyes in annoyance. "No. Dad calls to our *magic.* 'The pack alpha controls the energy of the pack,'" he quoted.

Cade and Gray stared at each other before turning their attention back to Garon. Gray's head swam with the new way of thinking, but Cade was full of questions. "So, Gray can call on Simon's energy, like he's a wolf?"

"Sheesh, didn't your teacher make you read the book?" Garon bit his lip and looked sheepishly at his dad. "Sorry. That was rude. I know."

Gray couldn't help but chuckle. "Yes, son, it was pretty rude. And yes, I clearly remember being forced to read the pack history when I was your age."

"Yeah, we all have to read it, even though it's old and boring some-times. It says it in there though. Well, it says energy and not magic, but it's the same thing, isn't it?"

Gray supposed to a ten-year-old mind it would seem like the same thing. His mind, however, didn't think of it that way. "I can see why you'd think that. I've never been taught that they were the same."

"Oh, they are, Dad. I know it. 'Cause when Simon got hurt, I just knew all I had to do was give him a little energy to help. The other kids knew it too, and they aren't even as old as I am."

Kneeling next to Simon on the floor, Gray realized he was willing to put his faith in his son's beliefs and try to pass some magic on to Simon. He glanced at Cade, who looked as confused as ever, but in the end, Gray trusted his son. "Let's give it a try."

Gray focused his energy on Simon and concentrated in the same way he would as an alpha to any wounded member of his pack. Garon's hand slipped into his. They each grabbed one of Simon's hands, forming a circle with the three of them as Cade watched from behind Gray.

"I can feel his magic, Dad. Can you?"

"Yes."

"Can you help him?"

Gray didn't know, but he wanted to try. He gave a little push with the energy of his wolf—not as hard as he would to a member of the pack but enough to make sure Simon didn't react negatively. Simon's energy connected with his own, but it didn't feel bad or hurt.

Instead, it seemed they completed a circuit. Gray's energy was a power cord; Simon's was the outlet. When plugged in, energy could flow freely between them. It was a strange sensation, different from healing a pack member but only slightly.

Gray thought about how he helped another wolf heal itself and sent that specific message through their connection. Simon gasped, his body trembling slightly. After a moment, he relaxed with a sigh. Gray disconnected, pulling them back, and let Simon's magic do the rest.

Garon squeezed his hand, and Gray looked over at him. "You did it. His magic isn't hurting as much now."

Before Gray could respond, he heard the front door open and running steps coming up the stairs. He tensed a moment until he recognized Aunt Maggie's scent. She burst into the room, ready to fight whatever was hurting her family.

Her eyes passed over them all quickly, taking in the scene with a glance. "Gray?"

He knew she was asking for an explanation. He gave her a quick rundown. She leaned down next to Garon and ran her hand over his head. Garon turned into her and nuzzled his face into her familiar touch.

She pulled him into her arms and hugged him tightly. "Sounds like you had an exciting night, young man."

He nodded against her shoulder and yawned widely.

"Well, let's get you into bed."

Gray helped her get his son settled. They tucked him in, and both kissed his forehead. Garon scrunched up his nose. "I'm too old for night-night love."

She scoffed at him and gave his shoulder a squeeze. "You're never too old for that."

Garon didn't argue and gave her a small smile as his eyes began to drift shut. "Dad?" he whispered.

"Yeah?"

"He's one of us now."

Gray knew he meant Simon, and had a brief moment of panic that somehow he'd turned Simon into a wolf. But that wasn't possible. He could feel Simon now, though, just like any other member of his pack. Simon was one of them in a way he hadn't been before.

Aunt Maggie met Gray's eyes over the bed, and he could see the tears in them. "I'll stay with him. Should we settle the mage in the guest room?"

Gray's instincts were to put Simon in the extra twin bed in Garon's room, just to keep them together where he could watch over them both. Garon needed rest, though, already drifting off to sleep.

"That's fine. I'll stay with Simon. You let me know if there's any problem, anything at all."

"I will, Alpha. I'll watch over him like my own."

Cade still knelt on the floor next to Simon. He stared at him like he had horns growing out of his head.

"Cade?"

"I can sense him. How is that possible?"

"I don't know. I'm hoping he'll be able to explain it when he wakes. I want you to stand guard downstairs."

Cade nodded and left the room with one last questioning glance back at Simon. Gray carefully lifted Simon in his arms and took him into the guest room. He pulled the yellow floral bedspread his mother had purchased for the room back with an awkward tug and wished for a moment he'd taken the time to redecorate. Then he realized how ridiculous he was being. Simon wouldn't care what the bedspread looked like. Gray lowered him to the cool sheets, startled when he felt a touch to his face. Simon was awake, staring at him with a dazed and tired expression. He brushed his fingers over Gray's jaw.

"It's soft. I thought it would be prickly."

"No, just a little prickly." Gray couldn't help but grin. Simon was clearly exhausted. Gray was sure he'd never be so forward otherwise.

"Hmm," Simon mumbled, "I never thought I'd like facial hair, but I do now."

"I'm glad," Gray replied. "I never thought I'd like a mage, but I do now."

Simon's eyes drifted up to meet Gray's, a sudden heat in them. "I'm glad, too." The heat shifted to terror as his memories came into focus. "Oh God, Garon. Is he okay?"

Gray ran his fingers over Simon's smooth cheek to calm him. "He's fine. You saved him."

Simon let out a slow breath. "I didn't know what I was doing, but I tried. What about the other kids?"

"They're fine. No trouble at all with them."

"Good. I need to check them, too. Just to be sure."

"You can, later. You need to rest now."

Simon placed his hand over Gray's where it rested on his face. "Will you stay with me?"

Their eyes locked, and Gray nodded. Simon moved over, and Gray stretched out beside him. He reached down and pulled the covers up over them. Simon slowly rolled to his side and wrapped his arm across Gray's chest.

"Is this okay?" he whispered.

Gray's answer was to cover Simon's arm with his own, holding it in place.

A DISTURBANCE from downstairs woke Gray moments before he heard Emma's voice in his head. *Alpha Gray, Cade is mean and won't let us in.*

He had to chuckle at the indignant tone. He heard Cade's voice drifting up the stairs. "Emma, I told you Alpha was sleeping. You didn't wake him, did you?"

"Yes, I did. Alpha said I could always call him if I needed help, and I need him to help me make you move. You're mean!"

Gray snickered and tried to extract himself from Simon's embrace. The mage was plastered to his side, their bodies entwined. Gray groaned when Simon wiggled his way closer. A crease formed on his forehead when he realized Gray wasn't staying still.

Simon's eyes blinked open. "Where are you going?"

"Downstairs. Cade needs my help."

Simon tilted his head to the side like he was listening. Gray realized he was, and that he could hear the ruckus going on as well as Gray could. He chuckled and looked over at Gray. "She's a feisty little thing, isn't she?" Simon moved his arms and legs and let Gray slip out of the bed.

"I'll be back in a few minutes."

Simon nodded and closed his eyes again. His breathing evened out quickly as Gray left the room and went downstairs to "help" one of his youngest pack members.

When he reached the bottom of the steps, he was surprised to see not only Emma and her parents, but also the other kidnapped kids and their parents as well. He'd been sleeping so soundly he hadn't heard them all come in. "Good morning, pack. What's the problem?"

Emma sent a superior look at Cade before she looked over at Gray. "Morning, Alpha! We came to help Simon, but Cade said no. That's not very nice. You should always help someone who's hurt, isn't that right, Alpha?"

Gray could tell Cade was irritated, but it was hard to argue with a five-year-old's logic. "Well, Emma, I suppose it is usually right to help."

Emma's father, Jeff, spoke up. "We're sorry to bother you, Alpha, but she got up this morning and insisted we come straight over. It looks like the others had the same idea."

The other parents nodded their agreement, and the kids all gathered together in front of Gray. Danny, at nearly nine, was the next oldest of the group. He stepped forward and looked up at Gray. "Alpha, we need to help him. It's like, well, our wolves or something are telling us what to do. What's that word?"

"Instinct?" Gray asked.

"Yeah. It's like that. Mom says that when I get bigger my wolf instincts will help me do the right thing and stuff. But it's telling me now to make Simon better, like before."

Gray was just as shocked as the rest of the parents at this news. It wasn't common for their cubs to show many wolf abilities until after their tenth birthdays. Garon was over ten, but even he was stronger than he should be. He'd partially shifted in the night when Cade angered him, something that really shouldn't be possible at his age outside of the full moon.

The fact that their wolves were guiding them now was something he would have to learn more about. Gray felt like he was in so far over his head at this point that he considered calling his father home. The problem was his dad didn't know anything more about this than he did.

"Okay guys, here's the thing. Simon is resting right now."

"No, I'm up." Simon's voice came from behind Gray on the stairs. The kids all ran for him when they saw him, and he met them at the bottom of the stairs, kneeling to allow them all access.

Emma wiggled her way to the front, and Simon lifted her up with one arm. "Hey there, little one," he said.

"Simon, I'm not little. I'm a big girl."

"You're right. You are a big girl. Now what's this about you needing to help me?"

Jessie, the other girl of the group, moved to Simon's side. "We know we can help. You're hurt again."

Blake, the remaining boy, nodded his agreement. "We know, Simon. We felt you, like before."

Simon looked as confused as everyone else. "Gray, what do I do here?"

Everyone's eyes shifted to the alpha. He ran his hand over his cropped hair and tried to think it through. "Okay, cubs. You can help, but just this once. We're going to have a grown-up meeting later and talk about all this."

The kids all reached out to Simon as before, resting their hands on him. Gray watched Simon's eyes twitch, then slide closed for a moment, before he opened them again with a smile. Gray could see that much of the pain that had been in them before was gone.

"Thank you all. You guys are awesome," Simon said.

"It's okay, Simon. It's our 'in-stinks.' Alpha said so." Blake nodded dramatically, and everyone had to smother their laughs.

9

Simon was amazed by how at home he felt in Gray's kitchen. Aunt Maggie bustled around the stove, flipping pancakes and stirring eggs. Garon manned the toaster, taking the pieces out and buttering them before popping new ones in. Gray was in charge of setting the big oak table in the dining room. Everyone else moved around as well, taking care of getting the meal on the table. Simon was told to sit at the counter with a glass of juice. He figured everyone could tell he was a bit overwhelmed by all the activity.

Growing up, meals in his family home were quiet affairs. His parents took turns cooking and cleaning up. During the meal, they discussed their respective days and asked Simon about his, then they all went about their business.

At Gray's, it wasn't like that at all. Everyone pitched in to help, even the other pack members. Little Emma folded napkins and placed them beside each of the bright white plates. Blake laid out the forks while Jessie and Danny handled the spoons and butter knives respectively.

Gray and Emma's dad had pulled the table apart and inserted several leaves into the center, making it stretch from one end of the dining room to the other. The other parents carried in extra chairs and put them into place. It was a well-oiled machine, a family.

And it was loud. Everyone talked and laughed over each other. Simon tried to keep up with the conversations around him but couldn't. He could smile, though, enjoying the feelings of happiness that flowed from everyone around him.

"Simon, doesn't the table look pretty?" It was Jessie, her long brown hair in twin braids down her back.

"It certainly does. You did a great job helping."

She blushed and looked down. "Can I sit with you?"

"Sure," he said, then lifted her up. She was wearing jeans and a light-purple T-shirt with some cartoon character on the front that Simon didn't recognize.

"I'm glad you're pack now. We missed you when you weren't here." Her voice was so certain, and Simon hadn't felt this wanted in a long time. His chest burned with a familiar ache for a family of his own.

"I'm happy to be here. You guys sure are loud, though." He grinned and tickled her side a little.

She giggled and swatted at his hand. "This isn't loud at all. You should hear us when the whole pack is together. They're so loud they made my ears hurt when I was little. Mommy said I cried sometimes, and she told them all to shush up."

"And did they listen?"

"Well, Mommy said they tried, but wolves will be wolves, you know."

"Hmm."

"Mommy said that it was really brave of you to save us. Daddy said they owed you a life debt. I don't know what that means, but it sounded bad. You won't make them give you a life debt, will you, Simon?"

"Nope. Your mommy and daddy don't owe me anything at all. But you owe me something. A big giant hug."

She grinned and threw her arms around his neck, squeezing him tight. "I like giving hugs. Daddy says I give the best hugs ever."

"You know, I think your daddy just might be right."

The room had grown quiet, and Simon looked around to see everyone watching. The adults were all smiling, and the kids were looking around trying to figure out what was going on. He turned back to Jessie but spoke a little louder so everyone could hear. "I think we're even now. That hug paid off any debt anyone here thinks they owe me."

Jessie's mother called her, and she hopped off Simon's lap and ran to her mother's side. Gray locked his gaze on Simon, an unreadable emotion in them that Simon tried to interpret. Before he could figure it out, Aunt Maggie was calling him into the kitchen. "Simon, don't just sit there like a lump. Get the eggs on the table. They're getting cold."

"Yes, ma'am," he said, very pleased to have a job of his own to do.

AFTER breakfast, Simon shooed Aunt Maggie out of the kitchen and helped Garon clean up. Gray went upstairs to get dressed, then disappeared into his office to make some phone calls. The rest of the group left for their own homes. Simon found he liked the domesticity of the chore and could imagine he was part of a regular family.

The dishwasher was loaded, the pans cleaned, and the counters wiped down, so Garon rushed off to do some important task that probably involved playing a video game. Aunt Maggie was vacuuming upstairs, so Simon was left on his own to look around Gray's home.

The living room had two large brown sofas and several matching chairs. Pale green walls held a variety of artwork, from the childish scribbles of a young Garon to framed paintings of mountain scenes. The side tables were clear of clutter, with only the occasional photo of Garon and Gray on them.

Simon paused by one and lifted it from its spot. In it, Garon and Gray posed with an older couple that must be Gray's parents. He could see the resemblance between Gray and his father and ran his finger over Gray's glass-covered face, remembering the feel of his skin under Simon's fingers the night before.

"Not prickly," Gray whispered in his ear, causing Simon to jump and spin around. He plucked the frame from Simon's hand and placed it back in its appointed position.

"Not prickly at all," Simon agreed once he'd caught his breath. He traced his hand over Gray's face again and shivered at the sensation of those short hairs against the calloused skin of his fingers.

Gray let out a quiet gasp, letting his head fall back and his eyes drift shut. He reached out, found Simon's sides, and pulled him a step closer. "Fuck," he groaned, "that feels so good."

Simon's eyes drifted to Gray's throat, where his Adam's apple bobbed as he swallowed. It was the forbidden fruit, and Simon couldn't resist taking a bite. He kissed it first, then licked and nibbled over that little nub as Gray pulled him closer until they were fully against each other.

He continued to explore Gray's neck, his stubble rough against Simon's lips. Simon didn't care; he just enjoyed the taste of him. Gray moved his hand up to Simon's neck, holding him in place for a moment before pulling him away.

"Come into my office with me?"

Simon nodded, and Gray took his hand and led him into the other room. Once the door closed behind them, he pulled Simon close again. "I've been wanting to do this since last week," he said.

Simon didn't have time to breathe before Gray's mouth was on his, demanding Simon open to his questing lips and tongue. Simon trembled, and he grabbed hold of Gray's arms for balance. Gray guided him against the door, the solid wood at Simon's back giving him the extra support he needed. Simon broke away, gasping for needed air.

Gray attacked his neck, his beard rubbing against the sensitive skin, while Simon shivered and arched into the touch. Simon lifted his hands to hold Gray's head in place—there, at that spot that sent chills down his spine—and all his blood rushed to his now throbbing cock.

He arched his hips and pushed into Gray. Gray pushed back, his own dick hard and hot. He groaned against Simon's neck at the contact, and the sound vibrated through Simon's body.

Simon gasped, then grabbed Gray's shirt and pulled it up, revealing his lightly furred chest. He rubbed against it, wanting to feel the sensation against his skin. Seeming to sense his need, Gray pulled Simon's T-shirt up and off before crushing them together again. They kissed again, pressing their lips together, as Gray spun him around and moved Simon farther into the office.

Gray helped Simon down to the floor, onto a wool rug that teased the skin of his back. He raised up, pulled his own shirt off, and then lowered himself onto Simon. Their next kiss was slower, gentler, but had more heat than Simon could process.

His body was going up in flames, and he spread his legs to allow Gray to settle more deeply into the cradle of his hips. Gray broke away and traced his hand down Simon's body to the waistband of his pajama pants. "Can I?" he asked, his voice a husky whisper.

"Please," Simon said, "touch me."

Gray pulled the pants down to Simon's thighs, taking his boxer briefs with them. The cool air against his erection made Simon groan. Gray didn't leave it uncovered for long. He wrapped his big hand around Simon's length and stroked. Simon was sure his expression must be guiding Gray, his face showing when Gray had the right tightness, the perfect rhythm.

Simon reached for Gray's head, curling up so he could grab him and pull them back together. Gray continued his motion, but only kissed Simon briefly before beginning to explore his neck and chest. He paused at each pink nipple, sucking them into his mouth and licking around them until they were firm peaks.

He moved farther down Simon's body, giving each muscle on his chest attention before drifting lower to Simon's stomach. Simon sucked in his breath and pulled his stomach in as the hair on Gray's face tickled then pleasured him.

By the time Gray reached his cock, Simon was nearly out of his mind with pleasure. Gray teased all around, licking and nibbling everywhere but the spot Simon most wanted him, before he finally took the dark head between his lips. Gray teased at the slit with his tongue, tasting the drops of precome that leaked out, then took Simon deeper, engulfing his length.

Simon couldn't help but thrust deeper, but Gray grabbed his hips and pushed them back to the floor. His instincts were to keep trying, but Gray's big hands held him still while he continued to use his mouth to pull Simon closer to the edge.

The pressure built, closer and closer. Simon wanted to warn Gray, knew it was rude not to, but he was out of his mind. He didn't have to worry. Gray knew and pulled away, then scrambled to pull his jeans down his thighs before coming back to Simon.

Gray grabbed both their cocks and stroked them together. Simon tossed his head back and forth, finding purchase for his hands on Gray's shoulders. He squeezed, desperate to fly apart but not wanting this moment to end. He pushed his hips up, and up again, into the tight hold Gray had on him.

Finally, it was too much, and come exploded from his cock, leaving a trail of sticky fluid over Gray's hand. Another stroke and another stream of come burst from him. He cried out, couldn't stop himself, and heard Gray reach his own crest above him. Wet heat covered Simon, and he released his hold on Gray's shoulder so he could wrap his hand around Gray's as the strokes slowed to a stop.

Gray twitched and jerked above him, his head thrown back and his eyes closed. When he opened them and looked down at Simon, he grinned, gasping for breath. "Fucking hell, that was perfect."

Simon was beyond speech, but he nodded his agreement and released Gray's hand to rub at the dampness on his stomach. Gray watched Simon's fingers swirl through the trails then lift to Simon's mouth. He sucked in one finger, then a second, tasting their combined juices.

Gray grabbed Simon's hand, jerked it free of his mouth, and brought it to his own, where he tasted Simon's palm as well. They both groaned, and Gray lowered himself completely, finding Simon's mouth again.

Their kiss lingered, sharing the flavor of each other. After a few moments, Simon regretfully had to give Gray a little shove off to the side. The alpha had taken his breath away and was squishing him so he couldn't get it back.

Gray lay down on his side, supporting his head with one arm while the other trailed over Simon's body. "Can you talk yet?" Gray smirked, his cockiness making Simon chuckle. He shook his head, although he could have responded. "Glad to know how to shut you up, then."

Simon laughed out loud and punched Gray's shoulder lightly. "Be quiet. You're ruining the moment."

"Nothing could ruin that."

Simon had to agree. "I'm a mess. I need to get cleaned up." He paused, realizing he didn't have anything to change into. "I should probably go home and get dressed."

Gray grumbled and threw one arm and a leg over Simon's body. "You aren't going anywhere."

"Come on, Gray. It's not like you have something that will fit me."

"Fine. I'm coming with you, though. And you're coming back here so we can talk to the pack later."

"Oh, really?" Simon arched an eyebrow, not enjoying being ordered around.

Gray glared at him a moment, then relaxed. "I'd like to come with you so we can talk privately. Then I'd like for you to come back here so we can talk to the pack."

"Better, and that sounds good. I really don't want to meet any more of the pack in last night's pajamas."

10

*G*ray waited in Simon's living room while Simon showered and changed clothes. Although their styles were different in many ways, Gray felt really comfortable in Simon's space. Books, vases of flowers, and bowls of crystals covered the pine tables. Full-sized sofas like Gray's wouldn't fit in the room, but the denim-covered love seat fit perfectly in the space.

A beige recliner sat at an angle nearby, and Gray realized Simon spent most of his time there. The table beside it held multiple books, most with little slips of paper sticking out, marking pages. A coaster lay beside the books with an empty mug on top.

Gray sat in the chair, tempted to kick back and prop up his legs. Instead, he picked up the top book and opened it to the first of several marked pages. An herbal remedy guide, the page described natural treatments for headaches. Gray flipped to the next marker and saw cures for stomach problems.

He raised his eyes and looked toward the bathroom where Simon had disappeared a few minutes ago. With everything that had gone on, Gray wondered how affected Simon was from the demon attack. He seemed to be doing fine since the cubs had helped him, but it still bothered Gray to know he'd been here alone for a week, obviously not feeling well if his research was any clue.

The shower turned off, so Gray closed the book and put it back in place. No need to be caught snooping. A few minutes later, Simon came into the room, drying his hair with a damp towel. He only wore a pair of loose-fitting jeans, and Gray wanted nothing more than to give them a little tug and watch them fall. Simon caught him staring and grinned at Gray, and Gray couldn't help smiling back at him. "Feeling better?"

"Yeah. Clean and shiny." He chuckled and continued toweling his hair. "You want something to drink?"

"Sure."

Simon went into the kitchen and grabbed glasses from the cabinet. Gray sat on a barstool at the counter and watched him move through the space. The ice clinked in the glasses, then he poured tea. He plucked a sprig of mint from a pot in the window and let it float in the drinks before he handed one over to Gray.

Gray took a sip, then another, trying to identify the unique flavors. "What is this? It's good."

He looked up to see Simon smiling again, as if he enjoyed Gray's puzzled expression. "It's an herbal tea with lemongrass, mint, and a few other secret ingredients. My grandfather taught me how to make it."

"Mmm," Gray said after he took another drink. "I didn't think I'd like something like this."

"Well, I never thought I'd spend the morning fooling around on your office floor. Looks like we both found something new to like today." Simon winked and took a sip of his tea as Gray burst out laughing.

He reached for Simon's hand and pulled him around the counter, spinning his stool so Simon fit between his legs. "You are too much, mage."

"As are you, wolf," Simon whispered as he lowered his lips to Gray's.

He couldn't get enough of Simon's kisses. They intoxicated him, made him want things he'd never wanted before. Unfortunately, some pretty major obstacles stood in their way. When Simon broke away from Gray, he straightened his spine and took a deep, fortifying breath. Gray could see he wanted to say something but hadn't found the words. He brushed a finger across Simon's forehead, smoothing away the worry line that had appeared. "Hey, what's wrong?"

"There's something I have to tell you."

"Okay."

"I told you the other day when you came by that it wasn't good for us to spend time together." Simon stepped back, seeming to need some space between them. "I didn't tell you the entire truth."

"What does that mean exactly?"

"When I made the decision to rescue the cubs, I knew there would be consequences. I don't know what the rules are for packs, but for mages, we are forbidden from being involved with other magical beings. Because I broke that rule, I was reported to the Conclave."

Gray looked puzzled. "So will there be a fine or something? When a pack member breaks a rule, the pack is usually fined for a first offense, depending on the severity. This can't be that bad, Simon."

"You don't understand. There aren't fines in our world, at least not that I've ever heard. I'll be forbidden to have any more access to any mages, and I have no idea what they'll do to my magic."

"What? You've got to be kidding me. You saved children. It's not like you were out cavorting with the enemy or something."

"I don't know that they will see the difference. The master who is training me told me the consequences could be severe. He was extremely concerned."

Gray stood up and closed the distance between them. He pulled Simon into his arms and held him tight. "So the fact that you saved Garon last night is going to make it even worse for you."

"Yes. But I don't regret it, Gray. I swear to you I wouldn't change a thing. Your son is amazing, and so are you. I hope it doesn't come down to me losing the thing I've dreamed of since I was young, but if it does... well, I don't know what I'll do, to be honest. I wouldn't change my decision, though. I wouldn't walk away from any child in need."

"They'll understand that. They have to understand that."

Simon sighed and laid his head against Gray's chest. "I hope so."

They stood there for a long moment, Simon squeezing Gray to him, seeming to relish his strength. After a moment, Gray raised his hand to Simon's face and tilted his head back. "There is another way."

"What? I'm open to suggestions here."

"I can claim you, make you a full member of my pack. Then you'll fall under my protection, not the Conclave's."

Simon pulled back farther. "What? I don't understand."

"Look, I know we've only known each other a week, but I know there's something between us, Simon. I felt it the first moment I saw you, and I feel it even stronger now. I will make you my mate, right here, right now, and we'll go to the Pack Council for protection."

"Gray, no."

Gray grabbed his arms, forcing him to stay when Simon tried to pull farther away. "Listen, I know this sounds crazy, but I don't want you to sacrifice everything because of me, because of us. What you did was the most incredible thing anyone has ever done for me. You brought my son home and saved his life not once, but twice. Simon, please, just consider it."

"God, I don't even know where to start. I don't even know what it means to mate with a wolf. I mean, it's not like it is in the fairy tales, is it? You don't see your mate and immediately know that they are the one."

"Don't I wish. No, we meet and fall in love just like everyone else. The difference is that once we choose our mate and our mate accepts, it's for life. That's it for us; there is no going back."

Simon shivered and placed his arms on Gray's sides. "I can't believe you're willing to do that when you've only known me for a few days."

"I can't either. It's crazy. I'll admit it. But I'd rather take a chance on us than risk you losing everything."

"You are amazing. God, I don't even know anything about you, like your favorite color—"

"Gray, obviously."

"Or what kind of music you like—"

"Classic rock, but it varies depending on my mood."

"Be serious! We don't know each other well enough to make this kind of commitment. I love that you offered. I'm blown away. But I'm not ready to make that kind of decision, and I don't think you really are either."

"Simon—"

"No, Gray. You have to stop and think about this. I made the decision, and now I have to face the consequences. Maybe it won't be so bad. They might understand. This might just go away after a hand slap. I don't know."

Gray lowered his forehead and rested it against Simon's. "You don't believe that. Don't lie to me."

"I won't. I promise you. And you're right, I don't really believe that I'll get off without any type of punishment. But Gray, I still have a chance of becoming a mage. It's what I want. What I've dreamed of for so long, and I'll know in the next week whether it's going to happen or not anyway."

"They'll decide that fast?"

Simon shook his head. "No, I doubt it. My twenty-fifth birthday is coming up. If I haven't reached full mage status by that time, then this is all pointless anyway. My apprenticeship will be over. I want to try, though. No, I want to do more than try. I have to fight for this. Please tell me you understand that."

"I do. If someone told me I wasn't going to become an alpha, I would have fought for it. It's what I'm meant to be."

"Exactly. But it doesn't mean that I don't care about you. I do, more than I understand. Your pack, your family, has made me feel something I never thought I'd feel. If you had asked me a week ago if I would fall for a werewolf, I would have laughed at the idea. Now, I look at you and see something I want very much."

Gray nodded, rubbing his head gently against Simon's. He kissed

Simon's forehead and pulled back to stare at him. "Okay. I still want to see you though. I'm serious about that. I wasn't just saying I felt something for you to try to convince you to be my mate."

"I believe you. I feel something for you too. We can work something out. I'm not ready to walk away from you yet."

They kissed again, this time short and sweet.

Gray broke away first and traced a finger over the reddened skin around Simon's lips. "I suppose I should shave. My beard is scratching you all up."

"Don't you dare."

They both laughed and shared another quick kiss.

"I don't want to cause trouble for you, but we don't know anything about demons, and right now, you're our only connection to the one that attacked the cubs. We don't know how it got in or how to protect ourselves against it. What if it tries to go after Garon or the other cubs again?"

"I understand what you're saying, Gray, but the thing is, I didn't know what I was doing when I went up against it. My instincts led me there and helped me save them. I don't have the answers to your questions, and I honestly don't know what I can do to help. With this Conclave meeting hanging over my head, I could make things worse for both of us by staying involved."

It frustrated Gray to admit Simon had a point. He'd already said he had limited knowledge of Others, but Gray's instincts told him to keep Simon close. On the other hand, he didn't want to add to Simon's problems. Gray decided he had to figure out a way for them to meet in the middle. "This is getting more complicated by the minute, isn't it?"

Simon leaned into him and nodded. "I want to help, but this is all so confusing. I don't know what to do."

"It's okay, Simon. I don't want to cause you any more problems, and if associating with the pack is going to do that, maybe you shouldn't come to the meeting tonight. Besides, I know you're here if we need you or have questions."

Simon tilted his head to the side and looked into Gray's eyes as if searching for some clue. Gray kept his gaze steady, showing Simon he didn't need to be reluctant. Simon seemed to find the answer he sought, because after a moment, he nodded. "Okay. I'm sorry you had to wait around here for nothing."

Gray ran his finger over Simon's cheek and smiled. "It was worth it," he said and kissed Simon again to prove it. "Okay. The full moon is this weekend, so I'll be tied up with the pack. Can I call you on Monday?"

"Absolutely."

"If you need me before then—"

"I'll call. I promise."

Leaving Simon behind was one of the hardest things Gray had ever done. Every instinct screamed at him to turn around, go back and get Simon, and bring him to the compound where he would be safe. Gray knew he couldn't do that, and it made the drive home difficult.

The drive was nothing compared to the icy reception he received from his family when he returned alone. Aunt Maggie and Garon both glared at him, demanding to know where Simon was. He tried to explain, but they weren't having it. Garon threw a tantrum and had to be sent to his room. His bedroom door slammed behind him so hard the windows rattled.

Aunt Maggie retreated to the kitchen, where pots and dishes started clanging with alarming ferocity. He decided she was the lesser of two evils and followed her. "Auntie, I couldn't force him to come."

She gave him *the look*.

"Okay, I could have forced him. But what kind of person would that make me? Not the man my father raised, I know that much."

She huffed and rearranged the contents of the cabinets.

"It has to be his choice. He wants to be a mage, and if he stays here, he gives up the dream he's had his entire life. He just needs a little time."

She slammed a tin can down so hard Gray thought he might have to replace the cabinet shelf. "A little time? How much is a little? And what happens if we need him again? What if something happens to Garon or the cubs?"

"I'll get him here as fast as I can."

She hmphed at him and straightened out the cans she'd knocked over. "Well, he needs to be here. He's family now. Family stays together. It's the pack way."

"I know, Auntie."

"That boy needs a family."

"Yes."

"And this is it."

"Agreed."

"Those mages hurt my boy, and they'll be facing me."

"And me." They both jumped at the voice behind them. Garon stood in the doorway to the kitchen with a determined look on his face. "They won't hurt him, will they, Dad?"

"No, son. Not if I can help it."

"They better not, or it'll piss me off."

"Garon! Language!"

"I'm sorry, Aunt Maggie, but Dad says that sometimes you just need a bad word to make your point, and I mean it."

Gray tried not to laugh. "It's fine this time, but watch it, okay?"

"Okay. Dad, can you help me with my math homework? Cade brought up my work for me today since I couldn't go to school 'cause of being up most of the night."

One of the mothers had stepped into the role of teacher while Valerie recovered. Although she'd regained consciousness on her own, she wasn't ready to go back to teaching classes yet. Her husband was keeping Gray updated on her condition, and he knew from their link she was having terrible nightmares. She'd called out to him several times in the past week for help, only to wake up and apologize. Gray kept assuring her it was okay, but he didn't know if she'd ever be able to teach again.

In the meantime, he had to keep Garon moving forward with his studies, as much as his son hated doing his homework. "Sure, kiddo.

Let's go into the office. Those multiplication problems still giving you trouble?"

"Yeah. Stupid sevens. I can't remember them. Who needs sevens anyway?"

Gray winked at Aunt Maggie and followed Garon into the office. Several hours passed relatively quietly before the pack members began to gather for the meeting that evening.

Cade and Liam arrived first, followed by one parent of each of the cubs involved. The pack elders entered last, including Aunt Maggie, who set several trays of food around the crowded living room before taking a seat beside Gray on the sofa. Liam, as his beta, sat on his other side.

Gray waited a moment, his ears focused upstairs for the distinctive noises that came from Garon's favorite racing video game. He heard the crashes and Garon's laughter and knew his son was distracted for the time being.

"Tonight we're here to discuss what's going on with the cubs." It seemed so simple to say it that way, when they all knew the situation facing their pack was very critical. Gray recapped what he'd learned so far and let the other parents describe the effects their cubs were experiencing.

The elders asked several direct questions to clarify points beyond what Gray had explained to them previously. It didn't take long for the conversation to turn to Simon.

Gray fielded the questions as best he could before Aunt Maggie stepped in to help. "We need to give him some time. Those of you here this morning for breakfast saw as well as I did that he didn't know what to do with all of us."

Jessie's dad spoke up. "That's true. He didn't seem to know how to act in a family."

Aunt Maggie nodded. "Exactly. Now we just have to give him time. He's"—she looked at Gray— "one of us now. We take care of our own."

Cade leaned forward in his seat. "I agree. At the least, he's earned our protection."

Everyone nodded their agreement. Gray was glad they all wanted to keep Simon safe. He felt the same. "What do you suggest?"

It was Liam's turn to add to the discussion. "I think we should alter the new guard routine and add Simon's place to the schedule."

"We can do that," Cade said. "I've got plenty of volunteers for guard duty since this all happened, and I don't think anyone would mind."

Jackson, one of the elders, ran his hands through his nearly white hair. "I hope we know what we're getting ourselves into with this. Gray, what has the Pack Council said?"

"Not much, Jack. They're looking into it. Same as they were last week. No one seems to know what to think of all this, that's for sure."

They all seemed at a loss. None of them knew anything about mages or their magic either. In the end, the only thing they all agreed on was that Simon should be watched over.

11

On Monday morning, Simon gave his stomach a quick rub as he worked on weeding the flower beds in his backyard. Two trays of impatiens waited beside him, ready to be planted, but he had to get the beds cleared first. As he thought about the best place to get mulch this year, his stomach sent another pang of warning to him.

His body ached again but nowhere near as badly as before the cubs had helped him. The reactions to the negative energy he'd absorbed worried Simon. The dark spell inside him remained trapped in the bubble he'd created around it.

Digging out a stubborn weed, Simon focused on the darkness for a moment. It seemed to be growing weaker, which Simon thought was a good sign. With no clue how to get rid of it himself, he dreaded asking Master Thomas for help.

He would have to get over his apprehension before their regular training session, scheduled for later in the morning. Simon had already meditated, finding it easier than before to center himself. It surprised him, especially considering everything he'd been through over the weekend.

He wiped his sweaty face on his grime-covered T-shirt, the last slightly clean spot now covered in new lines of dirt and sweat. The heat was menacing, even though it was still relatively early in the day, and the humidity thickened the air to uncomfortable levels. He decided to take a water break and try to cool down a little before he continued working in the garden.

With a little concentration, he could feel the presence of a pack member close by. Someone had been near all weekend. It seemed Gray had decided not to leave him completely alone. Instead of annoying him, it made Simon feel safe to know he was being watched over. Depending on someone else was a novel feeling for him. Part of being a mage required an ability to be alone. Mage training demanded a solitary focus, broken only by the master helping the apprentice.

Because of Gray, someone hovered just a few feet away, and he found he liked it quite a bit. He wiped off his soil-coated hands and brushed stray mulch from his knees. Simon cleaned himself as well as he could for the moment, went inside, and grabbed two icy bottles of water. Carrying them back outside, he called out, "You might as well come on out and grab a drink. I know you're there."

A moment later, a sheepish-looking Cade emerged from the trees. "Hey, Simon."

Sweat dripped off Cade, his dark green T-shirt soaked. He had a camouflage bandanna tied around his shaved head, and it too was drenched.

"Hey yourself. Did you guys really think I wouldn't know you were there?" He handed over the water, and Cade rubbed it over his forehead for a moment before answering with a shrug.

"Well, we are trained for this sort of thing. How did you know?"

"I guess I could feel you." Simon paused, considering the oddness of that statement. "You know, ever since the other night, I've had this connection or something with the pack. It's strange. Oddly comforting, though."

Cade didn't seem too surprised. "That's what it's like being in a pack. You always know someone is there when you need them."

"And you don't mind it?"

"Mind being in the pack? No, but then I've never known anything else. I think it would be lonely not knowing they were there."

"Yeah. I can see that." Simon was all too familiar with that feeling.

"Don't you mages have groups or something? It seems weird that you're out here by yourself."

Simon shook his head. "Nope. We all stay pretty much to ourselves. I'm not really sure why, but that's the way it's always been. My grandfather was a mage before me, and he had this place. It's where he came to work."

"So his family didn't even live here with him?"

"No. They had a house in town. I was allowed to come here after my tenth birthday when I started developing mage magic of my own. No one else was allowed to come."

Cade shook his head. "No offense, but that just doesn't seem right to me."

"None taken." Simon thought it was pretty unusual himself. He saw families on television and in movies, and although he couldn't really compare them to reality, it would be nice to have something similar. He longed for a family of his own, maybe a big brother to hang around with or aunts, uncles, and cousins to visit during the holidays. Since his grandfather passed, he rarely saw his parents, and his grandmother had moved to a condo in Florida.

"So what do you do here anyway? I saw you out here this morning, but you were just sitting there with this goofy look on your face."

Simon tried not to blush but couldn't help it. He'd been able to center himself this morning as soon as he thought of Gray. And the thoughts weren't exactly pure. "I was meditating," he explained.

Of course, Cade must have noticed his pink cheeks. "Uh-huh. And just who were you meditating on?"

"Shut up." Simon could feel his face burning as heat crept up his neck and across his cheeks.

Cade burst out laughing. "I knew it!"

Simon punched him in the arm. "You know nothing, and if you say anything, I'll... I'll... curse you or something. Turn you into a frog."

Cade laughed so hard he doubled over. "You were totally daydreaming about my alpha while sitting in the middle of the yard. He's going to love that."

"That's it," Simon said, giving Cade a shove, "now you have to help me weed and get my flowers planted."

"No way."

"Yes, way. Come on."

Cade followed without any other complaint and continued teasing Simon while they worked on the chores. They finished the weeding and were halfway through the flowers when Cade tensed and looked up. "Someone's here," he said, jumping quickly to his feet.

"Oh, that'll be Master Thomas. We have training today. I guess you'd better go back to lurking."

Cade smacked him on the back and made sure to rub in the dirt from his hand with a smug smile. "I've got your back, Simon," he said with a laugh before he turned and jogged off into the trees.

Simon scowled after him, wiping off the muck from his shirt before turning to greet Master Thomas. His master came around the corner of the house with his usual beaming smile, his hands reaching out to Simon. He frowned when he saw how dirty Simon's hands were.

"Pardon the mess, Master. I'll go wash up, and we can get started."

Simon hurried inside and cleaned his hands, even using a little brush to quickly get under his nails. When he returned outside, Master Thomas was already seated in the circle, ready to begin. Simon sat across from him and offered his hands.

Master Thomas flinched before he could grab them. "Simon? What's going on?"

For once in his life, Simon didn't want to tell the truth. He wasn't so much worried for himself as he was for Garon and the pack if the mages found out more had happened.

"I'm not sure, Master. I have felt an energy drain since last weekend with the demon but was only able to isolate it over the past couple days. I was hoping you could help."

Master Thomas paled and jerked his hands away. "You have been tainted by the demon." He scurried out of the circle and backed away from Simon.

"But Master, I need your help. Please, what can I do to fix this?"

Simon reached out to Thomas, unable to stand being rebuffed when Thomas was his only hope.

Thomas tripped over one of Simon's potted plants in his haste to get away. "I cannot work with you any longer, Simon. I won't risk being afflicted as well. This goes beyond me. I will report this new development to the Conclave immediately."

Simon watched him run from the yard and heard his car speed away moments later. With a deep sigh, Simon realized his dream of becoming a mage was slipping further away with every day that passed.

He refused to give in to the depression threatening him. Simon focused for a moment on Cade's presence and drew comfort from knowing he wasn't as alone as he felt. Giving in to the fear and sadness that wanted to bear down on him wasn't an option. Thoughts of the pack settled him and calmed his nerves to a manageable level. He renewed his determination to keep fighting, no matter what.

His list of tasks altered as his mind scrambled to make sense of everything. Gone was the to-do list of things he needed to accomplish to become a mage. Achieving full mage status meant nothing if his magic continued to be affected by the dark spell. Without the guidance of a master mage, he didn't know how to complete the training anyway. First and foremost, he had to find a way to get rid of the leech in his magic on his own.

There was really only one resource open to him since Master Thomas had abandoned him. He didn't have any other contacts with mages, had never even spoken to another mage since Thomas became his assigned master over four years ago. Even if he had known another mage, they wouldn't be allowed to aid someone else's apprentice. No, if he wanted a solution to his problem, he needed to find it himself.

At least he had his resources. His grandfather's library was just inside, filled with hundreds of books he'd collected over his long life. Sure, Simon had promised he wouldn't use the books until he'd passed the apprentice stage, but Master Thomas had broken his promise to get him through his apprenticeship. Simon refused to go down without a fight, and if reading some books that were levels above his ability could help, he had to try.

Settled in his decision, Simon went into the library for a reason other than to dust and vacuum. Grandfather hadn't wanted an overhead light in the room, so there were lamps scattered about on various tables. Simon turned on the standing lamp near the door and let its glow spread throughout the room.

He crossed to the windows and opened the blinds. The sunlight flowed inside, the bright glow filling Simon with the hope of a solution. He opened the window, and the smell of his herbs began to drift inside. Soothed by the comforting scent, he turned back to face the room and took a moment to run his hand over the smooth wood of the oak desk.

Simon remembered his grandfather in this very spot, seated in his creaky old chair as he grumbled to himself. Whenever one of his plants gave him trouble or a concoction didn't turn out correctly, he would settle at the desk with a stack of books. With one of his leather-bound journals spread open beside him, his grandfather would make long pages of notes in his flowing script.

Simon felt even more peace settle over him. His grandfather would want him to use the books to figure out how to get rid of the dark spell inside him. He took a deep breath, and for the first time in a long while, looked over the shelves for something that could help. Of course, nothing immediately jumped out at him. There wasn't a book with big red letters that read "What to Do if Attacked by a Demon." He was convinced something here would hold an answer for him. He only had to find it. Simon grabbed a few likely books off the bookcase and settled into his grandfather's chair. He'd just started reading when he heard a quiet knock at the back door. Setting the book aside, he went to the door and opened it to find Cade there, waiting.

"You okay? I heard what happened."

"I'm fine. A bit relieved, to be honest with you. At least now I don't have this big what-if hanging over my head. I'm sure the Conclave will take action sooner rather than later at this point."

Cade nodded. "Yeah, he seemed pretty freaked. You sure you don't want to come out to the compound? I'm heading there now. Liam is here to relieve me, but we can have you out of here in no time."

"No. Thank you for offering, but I think I'll stay. I'm going to go through my grandfather's library to see if I can find anything helpful. If I find something, I'll let you guys know right away."

"Well, if you're sure, I'll get going."

"I'm sure. Thanks, Cade. Here, take a drink out for Liam. It's getting hotter by the minute." Simon pulled a bottle of water from the fridge and passed it over.

"Thanks, Simon. He'll appreciate it."

"See you later." Simon closed the door and leaned back against it. He would find the answers he needed. He just knew it.

BOOK after book was a bust. Nothing about demons, weres, or Others seemed to exist in his grandfather's collection. Simon had been through most of the shelves by the time the sun started to set. He flipped on another lamp and scanned through the books again.

He started to reach for a history book when he paused, remembering that his grandfather didn't keep *all* his books here in the library. His journals were out in the workroom, where he could easily take notes on his herbs and other projects.

Simon hurried to the room, enjoying the clean smell of drying plants in the air. It comforted him, made him remember all those days at his grandfather's side preparing the plants for drying, crushing them into usable bits, and storing them for later use. This felt right. If Grandfather didn't have an actual book on the topic, he'd surely taken notes over the years of his experiences and observations.

His notebooks were in an antique cabinet that had once served as an armoire. A faded mirror, speckled with age, still lined one of the doors. Simon jumped when he saw his reflection, a moment of panic overtaking him. He laughed when he realized he was staring at himself and not some stranger who'd come to steal him away.

Simon had kept his grandfather's habit of keeping the cabinet locked up, even though the key was hanging just inside the door of the room on a hook. He carefully got the doors opened, wiggling the key just so to convince the worn lock to release its hold, and stared at the pile of leather-bound books inside.

The gardening notes were separated from his general notes according to shelves. The topmost row held all his gardening secrets. But it was the next batch of books Simon was more interested in. He had never read his grandfather's personal journals, even years after his death. They were his grandfather's private thoughts, and he'd never felt right about reading through them.

Now, though, a shiver of excitement poured through him. The answer was here. He could feel it. His grandfather had left him these books for a reason, had insisted on leaving this cabin and its contents for Simon's use, and for the thousandth time, Simon was so grateful for his planning. He grabbed the first few journals and sat down on the floor. He flipped through the first one quickly, scanning the pages for any key words. Demon, werewolf, Other, dark magic. He looked for anything that could help. The stack of journals grew by his side as he flipped through year after year of notes.

Finally, Simon found what he was searching for. His mouth fell open in shock as he read, and his eyes filled with tears that rolled down his cheeks unnoticed. Simon couldn't believe he'd been so wrong for so long.

12

*M*onday morning was always busy for Gray, but this morning was unusually so. Rocky arrived with a mountain of security equipment and two of his team members to install the new system. Gray concentrated on the details and forced his mind to remain focused on the new safety measures.

He tried not to count down the minutes until they finished and he could call Simon. Gray had missed him over the weekend, more than he wanted to admit. He didn't know what it was about Simon that drew him in so completely. The connection between them excited Gray, made him think of possibilities and long-term plans.

The pack run rejuvenated him, and the rest of them as well. They'd all needed the time together as wolves and a pack to reconnect. Gray wished Simon had been with them, though. He thought Simon would have enjoyed seeing them in their wolf forms. The adult wolves could be a bit intimidating, but there wasn't much cuter than a group of wolf cubs.

Gray could imagine Simon sitting on the ground with a group of them frolicking around him and jumping up to lick his face. He figured Garon would lead them in pouncing on Simon's back and nipping playfully at his fingers. Lost in his daydream, Gray warmed to

i

the idea of Simon being there with them and experiencing the best they had to offer.

Unfortunately, now wasn't the time for him to get lost in that fantasy. Rocky laid out a technical map on Gray's desk, and Gray returned his attention to the task at hand.

Rocky wasn't what Gray had expected when he'd pictured a security specialist. Tall and thin, with pale white skin and shaggy dark red hair, Rocky didn't look like he would stand a chance against the larger wolves in their pack. Alex assured him appearances were deceiving, especially in Rocky's case.

He certainly knew his business, however, and Gray set aside his first impressions and listened as Rocky expertly explained the new security system. Wires would be buried at the gates and along the property lines. False wires provided an extra level of protection. If they were tampered with, alarms would sound. New cameras were set up, and both gates were monitored. It all ran together after a while, but Rocky was nothing if not thorough.

Liam had been there for most of the explanation. His responsibilities included the security of the pack, and he'd left only when it was his turn to watch over Simon. He'd nodded at Gray before he went, and Gray had accepted the gesture of reassurance that Simon would be looked after.

A little while later, Cade stormed into the office.

Gray didn't know what was up, but not much rattled his best friend. "What's wrong?"

"Those mages are pieces of shit, that's what's wrong. Do you want to know what that supposed master said to Simon? He washed his hands of him. Told Simon he was tainted and was scared he would be too. What a dick! He didn't even offer to help, just hightailed it out of there like Simon had the plague or something."

Gray couldn't believe it. That wasn't how things were supposed to be. A pack member would never be shunned like that. "What do you mean, Simon is tainted?"

"I don't know. Simon said something about an energy drain, and that asshole just jumped back and said the demon had tainted him. Do you think whatever he did to help Garon was what did it?"

"That must be it," Gray said. "I thought the cubs had healed him."

Rocky looked back and forth between them, his eyes widening. "Something else has happened, I take it?"

Cade sank down in a chair and clenched the arms with his hands. "You could say that."

"Anyone care to expand on that?"

Cade looked at Gray, who gave Rocky a rundown of the events. Rocky appeared shocked as well. "So this mage guy, who is the same guy who saved the cubs in the first place, comes back and saves the alpha-heir again?"

"That about sums it up," Cade grumbled.

Rocky shook his head and sat down in the chair beside Cade's. "You guys are in some deep shit here."

"We know," Gray said. "We're waiting to hear from the Pack Council, but this seems to be something that hasn't happened before."

"That's the understatement of the century. We've lived peacefully with the Others for as long as I've heard. My grandmother used to tell stories about the Others, the mysterious mages that we were to avoid, and how dangerous demons and the like were."

"Our elders say the same thing. No one has ever heard of a demon attacking a pack before, and certainly a mage has never come to a pack's assistance."

Rocky turned to Gray and seemed to have something to say but didn't speak.

"What is it?"

"Alpha, I don't want to question your judgment, but are you sure it's wise to keep the mage so close? It seems really suspicious to me that he conveniently showed up right when you needed him, that he was there to 'save the day.'"

Gray didn't want to admit Rocky had a point. Looking at it from an outsider's perspective, it did appear questionable. But there was something about Simon, something Gray trusted even though he couldn't explain it. He said as much to Rocky.

Rocky nodded, his expression unchanged. "And that doesn't bother you?"

"What?"

"That you just trust him like that, for no real reason. He came out of nowhere, Gray. I know you don't want to hear this, not after what he did for Garon and the other cubs, but I don't trust him. I don't know what his motives are, and I hate to say it, but I'm not sure that he hasn't done something to you to get you to feel this way."

Gray leaned back in his chair, his thoughts racing. He'd seen first-hand what Simon could do, how he'd used his abilities to control the humans who had kidnapped the cubs.

Cade slammed his hand down on the arm of his chair. "Enough. You don't know what you're talking about. You weren't there, man. You didn't see what Simon did to save Garon. I did. He would have died, killed himself to save our alpha-heir, for no reason other than it was the fucking right thing to do." He jumped up and went to Rocky, getting right in his face with a snarl. "Don't question us on things you know nothing about. If you had seen what he did, you wouldn't be saying this shit."

"Cade, enough." Gray's voice was sharp, and Cade turned, raising his fist to the wall. He reconsidered and put his hand down before he struck.

"See, that's what I'm talking about," Rocky added. "Look at how quick Cade is to defend him, how angry he is. You've all just taken him in, and, yeah, I get that he saved the cubs." He paused and looked back and forth between them. "But since when are we so trusting to outsiders? I'm not trying to be an asshole here, but you have to admit the whole thing is weird. Why would he do that? He's not pack. Cade just gave a perfect example of how the mages aren't like us. So what does he gain from helping you?"

"Nothing," Gray answered.

Cade let out a breath, still looking away from them and at the wall. "That's not entirely true." He turned and locked eyes with Gray. "He got some of your magic."

Rocky took in a shocked breath, his eyes wide. "What do you mean, 'he got some of your magic'? You left that out."

Gray stood up and paced behind the desk. "When he saved Garon, he depleted his magic. He was going to die, so I treated him like he was an injured pack member and tried to get him to heal."

"What the hell were you thinking?"

Cade growled, spun around, and stalked toward Rocky. "Do not speak to my alpha that way."

Gray didn't stop him. He was beginning to get pissed as well. "I was thinking that the man had just saved my son's life at the sacrifice of his own. I was thinking that he'd done nothing wrong." Gray stopped and came around the desk. He stood shoulder to shoulder with Cade over Rocky. "And I was thinking that I wasn't going to let him die."

Rocky lowered his eyes and tilted his neck to the side. "I'm sorry, Alpha. I didn't mean to be insulting. This whole thing is so far out of my experience."

Gray huffed out a bitter chuckle. "Your experience? How do you think I feel? I see what you're saying, Rocky, and I appreciate it. But here's the thing. I trust Simon. My son trusts Simon."

"We all trust him," Cade added.

"Bottom line, he's now a friend of the pack. He's hurt because he helped us, and we need to find a way to help him."

"Hey, he said he was going to go through his grandfather's books to see what he could find. So that's good, right?" Cade sounded so hopeful that Gray laid his hand on Cade's shoulder and gave him a gentle squeeze.

"Yeah, that's really good. We'll figure this out."

Rocky stared at them both for a moment. "Well, I still don't like it, but I trust you guys. If you trust this guy, then I'll leave it alone. Of course, this does open up a new issue for us regarding security."

"I'm not sure what you mean," Gray said.

"Gray, I can't be sure that this system will keep out the Others. It has never been tested against any magic outside the pack before. We're unprepared to defend ourselves against mages and demons."

MACY BLAKE & POPPY DENNISON

"Don't worry about it. I've thought about that, and there's nothing we can do but try. Bottom line, when the cubs were taken, the kidnappers disabled the existing security system. That tells me that they needed to, for whatever reason. Garon said to me the other night that magic is energy. The way you've set this up, if the energy is tampered with, the alarms will sound. All I can do is believe that and keep our guard up until this gets resolved."

"I hope you're right. You know, I wonder if this mage of yours would be willing to help with that. If he's willing to share information, maybe I can work with him and figure out some way to enhance the security."

"We can ask him." Gray sat back down behind his desk, resolved to find some way to help Simon. He couldn't sit by and allow Simon to be cut off from the mages, not when he was so close to completing his training. There had to be something they could do, some way to get themselves out of the mess they were facing.

He stared at the phone for a long moment and considered calling Simon, just to hear his voice. No, he'd wait a while, let Simon do what he needed to do, and Gray would find a way to spend time with him later.

Simon read the pages one more time before closing the journal and jumping to his feet. He hissed when all the blood rushed to his legs. He'd been on the floor so long they'd fallen asleep. The once bright light pouring in through the windows had dimmed to the faded ash of dusk. Waddle-limping toward the back door, Simon groaned with each step, even though he felt lighter than he had in weeks.

He wanted to tell Gray what he'd learned from the journals. With a laugh, Simon realized how much the alpha had invaded his thoughts. He leaned down to rub at his aching legs as the circulation began to return and knocked off a layer of filth from the morning's chores.

Changing course, Simon went to shower. The hot steam only increased his excitement. He scrubbed, his homemade blackberry and sage soap scenting the air as the suds covered his body. When he saw Gray again he wanted to look, and smell, his best.

He thought of Gray smelling his neck, his nose trailing down the sensitive skin there. Maybe he'd lick a little, tasting as he dipped down farther. Simon rubbed his hands down his chest, over his stomach, to his very interested dick.

Arousal surged through him when he gave it a quick, hard stroke.

After gathering a palm full of bubbles, Simon used them to slick the way and began a rhythm of pulls and twists that had his knees wobbling for a totally different reason.

Imagining Gray kneeling before him, mouth open to receive Simon's erection, made Simon arch and lean against the shower wall for support. He gasped, picturing Gray's hot lips and tongue around his dick, sucking and teasing at the slit.

With a groan, Simon shot his load into the bottom of the shower. All it took was a few thoughts of Gray's gorgeous mouth to bring him off. He stood under the steaming water for a few more moments, gathering his thoughts and his breath. He dried off and threw on a clean pair of jeans and a dark green T-shirt. He'd been told the color looked amazing on him. He hoped Gray agreed.

Shaking aside his lustful thinking, Simon restarted his journey to the back door. Once outside, he looked around for Liam. He headed for the section of woods where Cade had concealed himself earlier and heard a rustle in the trees to his right. Simon turned with a smile, expecting to see the pack member, but instead came face to face with a charging demon.

Simon didn't have time to react. The journal fell from his hands as the demon tackled him. They hit the ground hard, Simon's left arm twisting behind him. He cried out in pain and tried to struggle out of the demon's grip.

It was crazed. When Simon had last faced it, there wasn't this madness in its eyes. Before, it had been controlled and determined. This time it was out of control, set on its course, and Simon's fight didn't seem to faze the demon at all. Simon swung as hard as he could with his right arm, his fist connecting with a solid punch to the demon's jaw. It didn't even blink to acknowledge the strike. It grabbed Simon on either side of his head, sinking claws into the sensitive skin to hold him steady.

Simon threw up his shields, but it was too late. The demon was focused on the leech inside him, and for the first time in days, it pulsed with renewed life. He reinforced the bubble surrounding it, throwing everything he had into keeping that leech held tight inside the protective barrier he'd created.

One minute the demon was there on top of him, and the next it was gone. Simon heard a roar and felt the jerk of the demon's body lift from him. Stunned, he rolled his head to the side. Liam wrestled with the demon only a few feet from where Simon lay. It didn't even acknowledge Liam's presence. Its focus stayed on Simon and trying to get back to him.

That made it easier for Liam to fight it off. Simon cradled his sore arm against his chest. A few drops of blood oozed down his face from where the demon's claws had cut him. He tried to think of a way to help, to come up with some way to keep Liam from getting hurt, but he didn't know how.

Simon was beginning to panic, but after a few minutes of struggle, it stopped. Liam threw the demon, and it landed several feet away on the opposite side of the yard. Instead of coming back at Simon again, it turned and ran off into the woods. Liam started to chase it, but Simon quickly stopped him. "Liam, no! We have to get to Gray. It's important."

Liam growled, and for the first time, Simon noticed he was partially shifted. He looked like he was in pain, so Simon approached him. He winced and held his side. "You need to shift?"

He nodded.

"Go ahead. I can drive us."

Magic began to gather in the air. Before he had time to process the thought, a huge black wolf stood beside him on a pile of clothes. "You okay now?"

Liam's answer was to nudge at Simon with his head. Simon laughed and took the hint. "I'm going, I'm going."

He grabbed Liam's clothes off the ground, then hurried to the house. "Crap," Simon said, as he spun around to run back to the yard and grab the journal. Liam growled at him, and Simon could hear the "hurry up" in the tone. "I need to take this to Gray," he explained.

Spinning around again, Simon winced when his left arm suddenly began to throb. "Shit. That hurts." Liam was immediately at his side, his nose sniffing along Simon's arm. "It's fine. We'll worry about it later. Let's get out of here."

They went through the house, and Simon took a minute to grab his keys and wallet, then headed out the front door. The drive to the compound was strange with a wolf filling his tiny backseat. "I think I'm going to have to get a bigger car if I keep hanging around with you guys."

Liam huffed his agreement, his nose pressing into Simon's neck. "Cut that out. It tickles." Simon chuckled and moved his head to avoid Liam's snout. Liam licked his face, cleaning up the dribble of blood that traced down his cheek. "Seriously, Liam. Knock it off, you pest." Liam sighed and went back to staring out the windows, watching the darkness around them for any sign of a threat.

They arrived in front of the huge black gate after a few minutes. It opened immediately, and Simon started to drive through. A pack member he recognized as one of the cub's parents ran up to the car. Simon stopped, and he opened the passenger door and got inside. "Alpha is waiting for us," the man said.

Liam nodded and Simon drove again. He pulled up in front of Gray's house. The car was barely parked when his door was jerked open, and Gray pulled him into his arms.

"I'm okay, Gray. I'm fine."

Gray didn't seem satisfied with his words. He looked at Liam, who seemed to be communicating with him, then grabbed Simon's left arm gently.

"Gray, really, it's just twisted or something. It's not important. I have to show you what I found."

Simon pulled away and reached into the car for the journal. They started inside the house, and Aunt Maggie appeared, a towel full of ice in her hands. "Here, sweetie. Let's get some ice on that."

It amazed Simon how seamless they were. Garon ran down the stairs and threw himself against Simon. Simon held him tight. "I'm fine, little man."

"Don't leave again, Simon! You belong here with us."

Simon hugged him a little tighter. He wouldn't lie to Garon and tell him he wouldn't leave again. There were just too many stumbling blocks in the way for that to happen.

They settled in the living room, Simon and Gray, Garon and Aunt Maggie, Cade and a man Simon didn't know, along with Liam and the guard from the gate—it bugged Simon that he didn't know the man's name. He went over to him, holding out his right hand. "I'm sorry, but I don't remember your name."

The man smiled and shook Simon's hand. "I'm Robert, Danny's dad."

"Hi, Robert." Simon turned back to Gray. "And I don't know that guy either, but he doesn't feel like one of us."

"You're right. Simon, meet Rocky. He's from another pack, and I brought him in to help with security." Simon shook Rocky's hand, then went over to the couch with Gray.

"Is it okay to talk about what I found with everyone?"

"Yes. I trust everyone here completely."

Simon looked around the room. "You all need to understand that what I am about to share needs to be kept between us."

Everyone nodded agreement.

Simon opened the journal and laid it across Gray's lap with a smile. "I found something that might help."

"Might?"

"Well, I guess I should say I found some*one*."

"Simon, just tell us. I don't want to read all this now. Give me the rundown, and I'll read it later."

Simon grinned. "Okay, here it goes. A long time ago—centuries or something, it isn't clear—there was a vampire who had this brilliant idea to try to turn other magical creatures into vampires as well. My grandfather says that he was probably trying to build a powerful army or something." Everyone waited for Simon to continue. "So he hears about this one Enchanter who lives alone out in the woods."

"Simon, what's an Enchanter?" Garon asked.

"I'm not entirely sure, to be honest, but that's what Grandfather called him. So, the vampire goes to find this Enchanter and finds out the guy has a familiar." Simon paused and looked at Garon. "That's like a friend that's an animal." Garon nodded his understanding. "Well, this guy's familiar was a wolf, but not just any wolf. He was a werewolf."

Everyone gasped their surprise. "Exactly. So the vampire tries to be charming and convince the Enchanter that he should become a vampire so he can live forever. He offers to turn the familiar as well, tells them they will always be together."

"You mean so they can be best friends forever?" Garon asked.

Simon felt his ears heat up and cleared his throat. "Something like that," he said, looking Gray in the eye. The men were lovers, being offered a chance at eternity. Simon glanced around at the other adults and realized they'd caught the implication behind his words. "They said no, they weren't interested. The vampire waited and finally caught the Enchanter unaware. He attacked him, tried to turn him into a vampire, but something went wrong. It didn't work like it was supposed to.

"So the Enchanter goes crazy, hurts a bunch of people, ra—uh, does some other bad things, but finally, he comes to his senses. He goes back to his home and finds his lov—uh, familiar dead, along with the vampire who attacked them. Apparently, the vampire had tried to turn the wolf also, and it backfired as well. The wolf went crazy and attacked the vampire."

Gray stopped him. "Simon, how does this help us?"

"I'm getting to that part. So, the Enchanter slowly loses his humanity and becomes a vampire. It didn't happen instantly, like we read about in stories. It was a slow process, his magic fighting with the vampire's magic until finally he was a vampire.

"But nine months later, two little ones were born after his rampage. The new vampire felt so terrible about what he'd done that he swore he'd watch over the children. He did, and when they reached their tenth birthdays, they both developed magic of their own.

"He made sure they had the training that they needed, found other Enchanters to look over them. They grew up and had little ones of their own, the vampire always watching over them, keeping them safe. Eventually, one of the lines died out, as no children were born.

But the other carried on, generations of them, and he watched over them."

"Simon, come on," Cade grumbled, "tell us how this helps us."

"My grandfather was one of the children he watched over. And so am I."

Gray grabbed Simon's hand. "He's still alive?"

"Yes. My grandfather said he was scared of him at first, that he believed the stories about how they should all stay apart. And in some ways, he was right. If a vampire, or any other one of us, tries to forcefully change another, bad things will happen. But Grandfather believed that keeping everyone separated didn't have a real purpose."

"Cool!" Garon exclaimed. "So we can find this Enchanter guy, and he can help us, right?"

"Well, that's the plan, if you guys think it's okay. The thing is, vampires have soul magic, so if this guy is truly a vampire now, he'll have it as well. And the demon that is attacking us is doing it with soul magic. I think, *if* we can find him, the Enchanter can help."

Everyone started talking at once, the arguments growing more boisterous by the minute. Cade and Rocky seemed to be the most intense, yelling at each other. Even Garon was getting in on the act, his voice rising over the mix of the others.

Simon leaned into Gray, the loudness not bothering him as it had just a few days before. He felt relieved by it somehow, like he was one of them and they were looking out for him, like any other family member.

Gray released Simon's hand and wrapped his arm around Simon's shoulders and pulled him close. Simon looked up at him, and their gazes locked together. They stayed that way for several minutes, just staring while the arguing went on. Finally, Gray seemed satisfied and said, "Silence."

Everyone quieted and settled back into their seats. He looked at his second-in-command first. "Liam?"

"I'm in. I think it's clear we need some outside help, and this is the only lead we have."

Gray continued around the room. "Cade?"

"Count me in."

"Rocky?"

"I am not comfortable with this. I'd advise extreme caution."

"Noted. Aunt Maggie?"

"I think it's a good idea."

"Robert?"

"I agree."

"Garon?"

His son looked at him for a moment, surprised at being included. "Well, if Grandpa told me something important like that, you'd tell me it was the truth, that I should trust him. Simon's grandpa told him this, so I think it's okay."

"Good point, son." Gray looked around at everyone else. "So we're agreed. We'll contact the vampire and see if he can help. And we'll proceed with caution."

Everyone nodded their agreement, and Gray turned to Simon. "So how do we contact him?"

"I don't know. The only thing I can think of is to leave him a message at my house. He must be watching. Maybe he'll find it?"

"Okay. Simon, I'd like for you to come stay here for a while. With the second attack happening at your home, I don't think you will be safe there on your own."

"Okay. But only for a few days. Any longer than that, and I can't explain my absence to the Conclave if they come looking for me."

*T*aking a dozen fully armed werewolves in three SUVs to Simon's house was probably a bit of overkill on Gray's part, but he wasn't willing to take any chances. Six of his pack members guarded the perimeter of the house while the rest of them went inside to pack up Simon's belongings.

He watched as Simon looked around for a moment. Gray didn't think he knew where to start. Aunt Maggie stepped up beside him. "Let me get your clothes," she offered. Simon nodded and led her back to the bedroom. Gray followed to see if he could help.

"Just grab whatever, Aunt Maggie. There's a suitcase in the back of the closet. Let me get it out for you."

"Don't worry, hon. I'll take care of it. You go on and get the rest of what you need." She gave him a quick hug and shooed him out of the room. Simon waited until she put the suitcase on the bed, ready to pack, and started to open the dresser.

Gray took his hand. "Simon, let her do this for you. Come on." He led Simon back into the living room. Gray longed to hold him, but it wasn't the right time. He tried to ease Simon's worry with a smile and a quick wink. When Simon didn't respond, he gave Simon a little push. "What next?"

"Grandfather's journals." Simon ran his hand through his hair and sighed. "I don't want to leave them here. Just in case."

"Okay, we'll grab those," Gray said. "What else do you need?"

"Probably some of the books from the library. I don't know. I don't like leaving here. This is my home, Gray. I don't want to abandon it."

"I know you don't like it, but you aren't abandoning your home, Simon. It's just for a little while. We'll bring it all back, I promise. Once we know you're safe."

"Okay." Simon still looked lost, but it was all the encouragement Gray could give him. None of them knew what was going to happen next, but Gray wasn't willing to risk Simon being attacked again without the pack as protection.

Gray turned to Liam. "Go grab the boxes from the SUV and start in the library." Liam and Cade both left and returned a few moments later with the empty security equipment boxes they'd taken from the trash. They made a big pile in the middle of the room.

"Simon, any books you want me to make sure I get?" Liam asked.

"Um, some of the history books. And the herb books. Hell, I don't know."

"Don't worry, man. We'll just grab what we can." Liam left a few boxes for Gray, patted Simon on the arm, and went into the library. Cade and two of the other men followed him.

"Come on, let's grab the journals and get this done." Gray turned to the last wolf remaining in the living room. "Chris, keep an eye outside, and let me know if there's any trouble."

"Yes, Alpha." He moved to the front door to keep a lookout.

Simon led Gray into the workroom. Gray looked around at all the plants and herbs carefully labeled and hung to dry above them. More lined several shelves in small glass containers. Simon took a key off a hook inside the door and went to an antique cabinet. He unlocked it and handed Gray the stack of journals. Gray loaded them into a box, surprised by how many there were. They quickly filled the first box, and Gray started on the second.

When the cabinet was empty, Simon closed and locked it, even though there was nothing left inside it. He returned the key to its hook on the wall, then looked around the room and let out a breath. "I want to take some of my herbs too. Is that okay?"

"Of course, Simon. Bring whatever you need."

Simon pulled a small satchel from under one of the cabinets. It was made to carry the little glass jars Gray had noticed earlier. He loaded them up and seemed to be carefully selecting the ones he wanted on hand.

"Okay, I think I've got everything. We can come back if I've forgotten something, right?" Simon sounded completely heartbroken, but Gray knew he understood why they were doing this and that he shouldn't be left here alone.

"Yes. Simon, this isn't forever. You'll be back." Gray took the opportunity to pull Simon into his arms. Simon held on, and they stood there for a moment while the others finished their packing.

They returned to the living room just as Aunt Maggie was wheeling the suitcase down the hall. "I think I've got what you need, sweetie," she said. "I gathered up stuff from your bathroom too. You'll want to grab some shoes, though. I wasn't sure what you wanted."

Simon got one of his reusable grocery bags from under the sink in the kitchen and put a few pairs of shoes inside it. Everyone started loading the vehicles while Simon wrote the note for the mysterious vampire. He discussed with Gray what he should say, and they decided that vague was best. "Grandfather, I need your assistance. Please call."

Gray provided a cell phone number, and Simon added it before taping the note to the front door. As they left, Gray watched Simon stare out the back window, the pain in his eyes easy to see. Gray hoped it would be over soon, for Simon's sake if nothing else. He quieted the little voice in his head that rejoiced at Simon being with them, where he belonged.

WHEN they arrived back at the compound, Aunt Maggie led Simon inside while Gray and the others stayed out in the yard to discuss heightening their security measures. She took him to a nearly empty mudroom at the back of the house.

"Gray thought you'd be comfortable working in here, even if it is a bit small," she said.

Simon loved the space, even though it was different from the work area he used at home. The walls here were a sandy taupe, and the floor was tiled in similar tones. One wall was full of windows, and there were doors leading both inside the house and outside to the deck. He guessed at one point it had been a screened-in patio.

"It's great," he replied, smiling over at her. "I love how much light I'll get from the windows."

"Be right back," she said, and left the room, then returned a moment later with a broom, mop, and a bottle of window cleaner. Simon swept and ran a damp mop over the tiles, grimacing when his still-sore arm began to ache. He leaned against the mop for a moment to listen while Aunt Maggie wiped down the windows.

"This used to be where we kept the washer and dryer, but when Gray's folks modernized the kitchen, they made a dedicated laundry room on the other side of the house." She paused when she noticed him rubbing his arm. "You need more ice?" Simon shook his head, and she frowned at him a bit before continuing. "You should have seen the mess when they were doing all that construction. The kitchen was torn to bits, and Gray's mom couldn't cook for months while the remodeling was going on."

Simon thought the kitchen was amazing, so he figured the end result was worth a few months of hassle. It made him consider doing some work on his cabin, which hadn't been updated in years.

Since the remodel, Aunt Maggie explained, the mudroom had gone unused. It was too long and narrow for furniture, and when Gray added on the deck along the entire back of the house, they didn't really need it as a mudroom anymore. Everyone came and went through the back door into the kitchen.

They were finishing up the cleaning when Gray and the other pack members arrived with the first load of boxes. It didn't take long for them to get everything unloaded. They stacked everything along one wall so Simon could decide what he wanted to unpack. It narrowed the path that led from the side entrance of the house to the door that went into the kitchen. Otherwise the room was bare, save for an empty table that sat under the bank of windows.

"You'll have to let me know if there's anything else you need," Aunt Maggie said as she added the last box to the stack.

"I'll be fine," Simon replied, looking around the room. "Actually," he added, "a bookcase would probably be helpful."

"I think we can find one. There used to be one in here. I'll have to ask Gray where we stored it. I'm going to go on out there and check on everyone instead of using the—" She paused and tapped the side of her head with a smile. "Will you be okay for a few?"

"Of course. I'll get some unpacking done."

She left to go hunt Gray down, and Simon began looking through the topmost boxes. Now that he stared at them, he realized it was really crazy to have brought so much to the compound when he would be there for such a short period of time.

Gray came in a few minutes later, carrying an old bookcase from somewhere, and put it next to the kitchen door. Tall and thin, it looked like it was made for the space. "Mom used to put her laundry soap and stuff on here. It's not fancy, but I can buy you something else if you want."

"You don't have to do that, Gray. This is just for a little while, remember? I'll make do." Simon kept reminding himself that, for a short-term solution, the small space suited his needs perfectly.

Gray looked over Simon's shoulder into the boxes. With a smirk, he again offered to buy another bookcase for the room. Simon rolled his eyes and ignored the joking. "I didn't bring that many."

"You can bring as much as you want." Gray wrapped his arms around Simon from behind. He nuzzled that spot, the one behind Simon's right ear. Simon shivered when Gray's soft whiskers and softer lips moved as he spoke. "I wouldn't mind if you wanted to hang around for longer than a little while."

"You know I can't," Simon replied. He couldn't seem to force his actions to match his words, though, and stepped farther back into Gray, arching his neck a little to give him better access.

"Hmm," Gray groaned against Simon's neck. "Okay, but I want you to remember that you have options." He licked and kissed one last time before lifting his head. "You need any help with this?"

"No, I think I've got it. Thank you, Gray."

When Gray left, Simon turned his attention to organizing the stacks. He needed the distraction from his whirling thoughts.

Simon hadn't made much progress when Garon arrived home and offered to help. Garon was so excited that Simon didn't have the heart to turn him away. They worked as a team, Garon pulling the books out of the boxes and handing them to Simon, who placed them on the shelves.

After a little while, Garon started asking questions as he removed the books. "What's this mean, Simon?" He pointed to a stylized picture of a plant on the cover of a book.

"That's a book on apothecary medicine. That particular plant is used to help people who have a cut or burn on their skin. It's called aloe."

"Oh yeah, like the stuff you put on when you get sunburn."

"Exactly."

"I didn't know that came from a plant."

"It sure does. When it grows, the leaves get really pointy and when you cut off a piece it's full of this gooey stuff that you put on the burn, and it helps it get better."

Garon seemed satisfied with that explanation and handed the book over to Simon. "You sure do know a lot about plants. Do all mages study plants?"

"Not all of them. My grandfather loved plants and used them to make his own medicine, and he taught me how to do it too. I can teach you, if you like."

"That's cool. I bet they taste just as gross as regular medicine, though."

Simon chuckled and opened his satchel. He pulled out a container of dried rosemary and held it up to Garon, who sniffed it cautiously. "Hey, that smells like Mimi's pork chops!"

"This is rosemary, and it's great on pork chops. But it's also good for treating sore muscles when you use the oil from the leaves. Herbs and plants are used for lots of things. You just have to learn how to use them the right way."

By the time they finished unloading the books, Aunt Maggie was calling them in to dinner. Garon asked question after question about plants and herbs, then switched to asking about mage magic. When Aunt Maggie placed a large bowl of spaghetti on the table, Garon wanted to know what herbs and spices were in it.

Aunt Maggie blinked for a moment, clearly surprised by Garon's unusual question. "Well, I just used sauce from a jar, but I'm pretty sure it has oregano and garlic."

"Hmm. Simon, did we learn about garlic? I remember oregano. Wasn't that the one you can use for toothaches?"

Simon nodded. "It was. We didn't talk about garlic, but it can help with a bunch of different things. Problem is, it makes you stinkier than you already are."

"Hey," Garon protested, "I'm not stinky."

Gray put a pile of spaghetti and sauce on his plate and passed the bowl around to Simon as they all chuckled over Garon's response. "What else did you guys talk about, kiddo?"

Garon started to answer around his mouthful of noodles, but a quick glare from Aunt Maggie had him chewing and swallowing before he spoke. "Dad, did you know Simon knows how to make medicine that doesn't taste gross?"

"I didn't know that. That's pretty cool."

"Yeah, and he said that mages get a lot of headaches 'cause their magic is in their head and all, so he can make a poul—Simon, what's that word?"

"Poultice," Simon said.

"Right, he can make a poultice to put on your head that helps with headaches, and you don't even have to swallow anything."

"Garon?" Simon raised his brow, and Garon looked at his dad sheepishly.

"Well, Simon said that you still have to take gross medicine sometimes, and I have to do what you and Aunt Maggie say."

Gray nodded his approval. "He's right, Gar, but you know what? I'm willing to let you try what Simon recommends sometimes. But if you're really sick, you will still have to take what the doctor gives you."

"I know." Garon sighed. "Hey, Dad, do you think it's weird that mage magic gives you headaches? I mean, Simon says we have body magic that helps us shift, but it doesn't hurt. Don't you think that's weird?"

It was funny how kids could get right to the heart of a matter. Simon looked around the table. "It doesn't hurt when you shift?"

"No." The three werewolves at the table answered simultaneously, not a moment of hesitation between them. "Well," Aunt Maggie qualified, "it can hurt if the shift is forced, but that rarely happens. Our bodies know what to do and when we need to change."

Simon munched on his garlic bread as he thought. Perhaps his problems with his own magic were occurring because he was forcing things too much. It was definitely something to think about.

A ringing phone interrupted his musing. They all looked around for a moment before Simon realized it was the phone Gray had given him. He had left it in the mudroom and jumped up to go answer it. Gray followed behind him.

"Hello," Simon said after he pressed the correct button.

"Simon?"

"Yes. Who's this?"

"It's Cormac."

"Cormac, hi! I wasn't expecting to hear from you."

Cormac was a friend of Simon's grandfather whom Simon hadn't seen in several years. He traveled frequently, but always stopped by for a visit when he was in town. He often brought along some sort of interesting plant or spice he'd found. Simon remembered that his grandfather always looked forward to Cormac's visits.

"I just returned from a trip and stopped in to see how your apprenticeship was progressing. I saw your note on the door and thought I should call."

Simon wasn't entirely sure how to explain himself. "Well, things are a bit complicated right now." He tapped his fingers on the table in the mudroom.

"Apparently so."

"I'm not sure I can explain it to you, Cormac. I don't mean to be rude."

"Simon?"

"Yes?"

"I believe your note was addressed to me."

Simon's head began to spin, and he grabbed hold of the table in front of him. Gray wrapped his arms around him from behind and supported him. "It's you?"

His voice was low and weak, but Simon couldn't seem to make it stronger. He'd known Cormac for years and had visited with him on several occasions when he was a child. He had never picked up on any magic from Cormac, never once thought he could be the one they were searching for.

"Simon, where are you? Let me come to you."

"I, I don't—"

Gray plucked the phone from Simon's weak grip and switched the call so it was on speaker. "Cormac, this is Gray, Alpha of the High Moon Pack. Simon is under my protection at the moment."

"Alpha?" Simon could hear the anger and confusion in Cormac's tone. "Why on earth would Simon need the protection of an alpha? What is going on?"

"That's a very long story," Gray answered. "And one we would like to explain to you. However, I think we should meet somewhere else. I'm not comfortable allowing you onto pack grounds at this point."

"Fine. Come to me."

While Gray wasn't comfortable with that solution, they needed Cormac's expertise, so he agreed to the vampire's terms. Given his history with Simon's grandfather, they had to trust Cormac meant them no harm. Cormac gave Gray directions, and they arranged to meet later that evening. When he hung up the phone, Simon turned around in Gray's hold and wrapped his arms around him.

Gray held him close, whispering into his hair. Simon didn't listen to the words, but the comforting tone helped to soothe him. His emotions were spinning out of control. One part of him was elated they'd found Cormac so quickly and that the person they needed to talk to was someone Simon knew. The other part of him wondered how he could have missed such an important connection. How could he not have known who Cormac was or at least felt Cormac was something more than just a friend of his grandfather's?

Wrapped in the security of Gray's arms, he basked in the strength he drew from Gray's touch. Doubts began to creep in, though, doubts about his own judgment. If he'd missed something this important from Cormac for so many years, how could he trust himself to know what he was feeling for Gray?

ON THE way to meet Cormac, Simon tried to remember the last time he'd seen the vampire. It had been a long time, before he began his apprenticeship. Simon had moved into his grandfather's cabin the summer after he'd turned eighteen and graduated from high school.

There had been quite the fight with his parents over his decision. They wanted Simon to go to college, get a degree. More importantly, they wanted him to be normal, like they were.

Simon knew that wasn't for him. He'd known since he was ten that he was going to be a mage, just like his grandfather. The cabin was already in his name and had been set up in trust through his grandfather's will to be his. That summer, Cormac had stopped by to visit. It was the last time Simon had seen him.

Simon stretched his legs out in front of him and leaned back in a lawn chair. An ice-cold glass of lemonade dripped its condensation over his hand, and Simon lifted it up and rubbed the coolness against his forehead.

His grandfather's garden was a disaster. Part of the trust for the property had included a "caretaker," but it was clear to Simon the man had no idea how to care for anything. Sure, the maintenance on the house was fine. There were no broken windows or leaky pipes. But the garden, his grandfather's pride and joy, couldn't have been worse.

For nearly a week, Simon pulled weeds, trimmed shrubs, and raked leaves. Every day, from sunup to sundown, he worked to bring some semblance of life back to the grounds. The evidence of new life surrounded him, but he still had a long way to go.

He heard a car pull into the drive and knew he needed to get up to see who was there. With a small groan, he pulled himself to his feet and started walking around the house.

Cormac, his grandfather's friend, rounded the corner before he could get there. He was one of those guys who never seemed to change. Simon had only seen him a few times, but each time he'd been dressed in slacks and a nice shirt. Even in the heat of summer.

"Simon, I'm happy you're finally here."

His grandfather had shared with Cormac his plans to leave the property to Simon. "It's good to be here. Well, good in some ways. Bad in the amount of weeds." Simon chuckled and Cormac laughed along with him.

"Oh, your grandfather would have had a fit if he had seen this place the way it was not long ago. Can you imagine how angry he would be?"

Simon smiled and shook his head. His grandfather's temper where his garden was concerned was legendary. Greenhouses in the area shivered in terror when they saw him approach. Even mail-order companies were not safe from his wrath when his plants were not up to par. "He would have lost it for sure."

Cormac placed a comforting hand on Simon's shoulder. "I miss him very much."

"So do I. I always thought I would do my apprenticeship with him, you know? Even though he's been gone so long, I still think that he'll be the one training me. Silly, huh?"

"Never silly. You still have, what, two years?"

"Yes, sir. My apprenticeship officially begins on my twentieth birthday. I just turned eighteen a few weeks ago."

Cormac smiled and pulled a small package out of his pocket. "Oh, yes, the ever-important eighteen. I brought you something to honor the occasion."

Simon accepted the gift and slowly unwrapped the box. Inside, he found a crystal wrapped in copper wire and connected to a leather cord. Suddenly choked up, he lifted it out and held the necklace up in front of him. "It's just like Grandfather's."

"Yes, it is. I thought you would like to have one similar to his as a reminder of how much he loved you."

Simon nodded, unable to speak, and placed the cord over his head. The crystal settled several inches below his neck. After a moment, he could feel its warmth. "Thank you, Cormac. It's beautiful."

Simon was startled out of his memory by Gray grasping his hand. His other immediately went to his neck, but the crystal necklace wasn't there. Master Thomas had made him remove it during their first training session, saying it would mess up their ability to bond.

"You okay?" Gray's voice was quiet, and Simon nodded his answer. Liam stayed quiet in the backseat, seeming to understand just how upsetting Simon found the situation.

"I just can't believe that Cormac is the vampire, that he went through everything in the story."

"I'm sure he'll answer your questions," Gray said, giving Simon's hand a gentle squeeze. "Everything will be okay."

"I hope so," Simon whispered. He turned the possibilities over and over in his mind. The Cormac he remembered was a good man... vampire... whatever. Nice and kind. And he was family.

Simon felt a rush of pain at the memory of his grandfather's death. He clenched Gray's hand and tried to breathe normally. Maybe now that he knew the truth, he could be close to Cormac like his grandfather had been. Maybe they could be family now, especially since his own family wanted nothing to do with him since he didn't fit their vision of the perfect son. Simon's time with the pack, seeing what a family could be like, made him want that in his own life more than anything.

He looked over at Gray. Simon didn't know what this was between them. There was heat, lust, attraction. Was it more than that? Could it be more? Simon didn't know. One part of him wanted more. The other? It wanted to know if he could have a family of his own, maybe with his great, great—however many greats—grandfather.

*G*ray concentrated on following the directions Cormac had given him while keeping part of his mind focused on Simon. He didn't like how quiet Simon had become after learning Cormac was the mysterious vampire they sought. He could feel Simon's pain resonating through their bond and wanted nothing more than to comfort him.

All he could do was continue holding Simon's hand as he kept driving. Cormac needed to answer Simon's questions, and hopefully he had the other information they needed as well.

As he turned into the driveway of the address Cormac had provided, Gray tilted his head to the side and stared. He had pictured the home of a vampire as old as Cormac to be, well, as old as Cormac. Perhaps something dark and mysterious that kept out the sunlight. Something hidden away where he couldn't be found easily.

That wasn't the case at all. Cormac's home towered over the landscape, a newly constructed house with a vaulted roofline and a front facade made entirely of windows. It was built of pale gray stone, which of course Gray appreciated, but the outdoor lights and lush landscaping welcomed visitors instead of frightening them away.

Simon took notice as well. He sat up straighter and looked around in confusion and a little bit of awe. Even Liam leaned forward between the seats to get a closer look. There wasn't a fence or gate stopping them from driving directly to the front of the house, so that's what Gray did.

The dark wood front door swung open as Cormac rushed out, and Gray experienced another moment of surprise. The vampire only appeared to be in his thirties and had short, slightly curling brown hair. He wasn't even tall or commanding looking. Gray thought Simon probably had an inch or two over him in height. Not even his clothes gave a clue that he was old and powerful. His jeans seemed new, and he wore a plain blue T-shirt.

Cormac opened Simon's door and looked him over. Gray wasn't impressed with Cormac's obvious attempt to assure himself his kin was safe and secure in the company of wolves. Gray fought back a growl as he climbed out of the car and forced himself to remain calm. Liam followed, and together they rounded the car to join Simon, who still appeared to be in a sort of shock. Gray reached down and grabbed Simon's hand, much to Cormac's apparent annoyance.

Simon seemed oblivious to the tension, which was unlike him. From their first meeting, Simon had picked up on the emotions of those surrounding him, much like he'd heard the cries of help from the cubs. Gray thought Simon's sensitivity to others was because his mage magic made him more aware of the feelings of those around him. He reminded himself that Simon's magic was messed up and that Cormac was their only lead to help Simon get back to normal.

Gray gave Simon's hand a gentle squeeze, and Simon turned it slightly to lace their fingers together. The motion wasn't lost on Cormac, and his scowl deepened. He turned to Simon and tried to lighten the expression on his face. "Welcome to my home, Simon. I wish it were under different circumstances."

"Thank you," Simon replied, his voice still unusually low.

Cormac turned to Gray next and gave a brief nod. "Alpha Gray."

Gray returned the gesture. "Cormac. And this is my beta, Liam."

Cormac arched a brow at Liam, then turned back to Gray. "And you needed him here because...?"

Gray stepped forward, just one small step. Liam mirrored his gesture. The movement placed Simon just slightly behind and in between them. Gray then arched his brow right back, and Cormac nodded in understanding. "So that's how it is."

"How what is?" Simon asked from behind them.

Cormac smiled at Simon and gestured them all forward. "Welcome, all of you. Please come in. I find myself extremely curious as to what has happened."

The entrance hall had two doors that led deeper into the house. Cormac led them across the marble mosaic floor and to the left. As they passed through the door, Gray realized why there wasn't more security. Cormac didn't need it. The magic protecting the doorway nearly knocked Gray off his feet.

With a gesture from Cormac, the magic eased, and Gray continued into the room. Simon seemed unaffected, but Liam rubbed his arm like he'd been punched. Gray felt the same. Cormac was much stronger than he'd even imagined, and there wouldn't be much they could do to stop him if it came down to a fight.

The inside of Cormac's home was the epitome of class and money. Antiques from several periods were placed discreetly around the main room. Framed paintings lit by fixtures in the ceiling decorated the walls. Gray didn't recognize any of them, but he had a feeling he should.

The room they entered drew a happy gasp from Simon. It was a library, but unlike any library Gray had ever seen. The books all lined one wall, but that wall stood about twenty-five feet high. A small ledge floated around the upper row of shelves, and a low black metal railing kept the intrepid reader from falling to the parquet floors below. A circular wrought-iron staircase wound up one side of the room, allowing access to the upper level.

Simon released Gray's hand and walked toward the books. He trailed his fingers over them and traced over certain volumes lovingly. He turned back to Gray with a happy grin, then continued his perusal. Cormac watched him with a pleased smile of his own. Gray had to fight back a sudden burst of jealousy. Neither he nor his wolf liked that someone else was making Simon so happy.

There was a pair of matching couches in the center of the room, and while Simon explored, Cormac gestured for Gray and Liam to have a seat. They sat and waited, Gray's knee bouncing out an impatient rhythm. After a few moments, Simon noticed them and hurried over. He looked at the empty space beside Cormac for a brief moment before moving over to settle between Gray and Liam.

Gray's knee quit jerking, his nerves soothed by Simon's show of loyalty. Simon's fingers took up its nervous beat though, tapping as his anxiety built. Gray laid his hand on Simon's leg, and the movement stopped.

"Simon," Cormac began, "would you please explain to me what is happening here?"

Simon nodded and began from the when he had first heard the cubs crying out for help. He made clear that his torn feelings on whether to become involved were due to his fear of breaking mage guidelines.

His explanation of the first demon attack drew an angry expression from Cormac, and Cormac's frown deepened as Master Thomas's reaction to the events were recounted.

"It's disheartening to see so little has changed over the generations of my existence," Cormac said when Simon finished.

"And that's not all," Gray added. "We're actually here for another reason Simon failed to mention."

"So you are not asking for my help with the Conclave of Mages?"

"No," Simon insisted. "I made the decision to help and am willing to face the consequences."

"Then what is it?"

Gray squeezed Simon's knee, and Simon let out a long breath before continuing. "The demon placed some sort of spell on Gray's son. Garon has some mage abilities and was able to contact me psychically for help."

At this, Cormac leaned forward, his eyes wide. "There is a wolf with mage abilities?"

"Yes, sir. He's only ten, so he's still growing, but I think he's going to be strong. Probably stronger than me, anyway."

"Stronger than you? That seems unlikely."

"Simon, tell him the rest."

"Well, I couldn't figure out how to get rid of the spell on Garon, so I took it into me."

Cormac jumped to his feet and strode over to Simon. He placed his hands on Simon's head and closed his eyes. "Oh, my. Simon, you should not have done that."

"I had to. It was killing Garon."

"Yes, it would have. You were right to come to me with this."

Gray tried not to get overly protective at the sight of Cormac's hands on Simon. He tensed, and Simon laid his hand over Gray's where it still rested on Simon's knee.

"Can you help, Grandfather?"

Cormac's eyes closed on the word. "I can help. You weren't supposed to find out about me yet, you know. I promised your grandfather that I would wait until you finished your apprenticeship before I revealed myself."

"Well, it doesn't look like that's going to happen now."

"Of course it will, Simon. The Conclave will not be unreasonable in this, especially since children were involved."

Simon shook his head. "Master Thomas said I've been tainted by the demon and refused to continue my training. I'll be twenty-five in a week and haven't been able to reach full mage status."

Cormac shook his head as well. "This makes no sense. None at all. I'm not familiar with this master of yours, but he's clearly new and uninformed. The Conclave will hear your testimony, Simon, and though you may have to perform some sort of annoying service as a fine, they will not prevent you from completing your training."

Gray was happy for Simon, but still didn't quite believe it. He wasn't sure where Cormac was getting his information, but from what Simon had told him, this master person of his seemed pretty clear on the results of his actions.

"Now, first things first, let's get this spell removed from you."

Cormac walked to the side of the room by the staircase and held his hands up to a door nearly hidden behind it. "Come along, Simon. All of you."

They followed, and Gray felt more magic in the air as Cormac removed another layer of protections from the door. Once inside, he understood why this room was so well guarded. This was clearly where the vampire did his work.

A large table was in the center of the room, cluttered with open books, notes, and vials of unidentified substances. Gray thought it looked like an evil scientist's laboratory, but he didn't feel any evil here. It was oddly peaceful, despite the jumbled piles around the room.

Cormac grumbled at the mess. "Help me clear the table. Carefully, please. Just put everything over there." He gestured to an equally cluttered desk. Liam gathered up a few books and carried them over. Simon inspected a few of the containers as he lifted the holder they were in and found a place for them.

Gray stood watching, wanting to keep his eyes on Cormac. Trust didn't come easily to him, and he was placing an inordinate amount in this person he'd just met. Simon was too valuable to risk, but if they did nothing, Gray would lose him. His options were limited. Either he allowed Cormac to help, or he stood by while Simon weakened further.

While the table was cleared, Cormac pulled a few old texts from the shelves. He mumbled to himself, opening drawers in an old apothecary chest that stood to one side. He pulled out a large crystal, closed his eyes, and focused on it for a moment before shaking his head and returning it to its place.

He looked back to Simon, then nodded and opened another drawer. This crystal was smaller and an eerie green color. "Simon, up on the table," he said, and Simon complied. "Go on, lie down." Simon appeared anxious but lay back. Gray slipped off his jacket, rolled it up, and placed it under Simon's head.

Simon gave him a grateful smile and reached out for his hand. "You're going to be fine," Gray assured him, even though he wasn't really sure about it himself.

Liam stood in the corner, watching Cormac carefully. He was ready to pounce if anything looked like it was going wrong. Gray was glad he wasn't the only one feeling the need to protect. Liam's instincts were good, so Gray kept his focus on Simon.

Cormac carried the green stone over and held it above Simon's head. He muttered under his breath when it lit up and then faded back to its previous color. "Damn it. What the hell is this thing?" Cormac didn't seem to expect an answer, so Gray didn't try to give one.

Cormac went back to the cabinet and stared at it for a moment then turned away. "I wonder—" He went over to the wall and pulled a jeweled dagger from its hook. Gray hadn't noticed the weapons before, and he growled when Cormac turned toward them with the blade held in his hands.

"Down, boy," Cormac said and carried the weapon over to his desk, where Liam stood. "Out of the way," he said, and Liam moved to the side, his body tense and ready to spring.

Cormac fumbled in the desk drawer and pulled out a smaller, thin knife. He used it to pry a black stone from the handle of the dagger and held it up triumphantly when it was free. "This is it." He tossed the weapon aside, holding the stone gently in his hands.

Crossing back to Simon, Cormac laid the stone on his forehead. It didn't light up or anything, but Cormac seemed pleased with the results. "Yes, yes," he mumbled. "Ah, perhaps some copper." Back to the cabinet, where he pulled out some copper wiring and snipped off a piece. He wrapped it carefully around the stone, once, twice, three times, then held it up again.

"That should do it." Back to Simon, where he returned the stone to Simon's head. "This may hurt"—he glanced at Gray as he spoke— "but it must, in order to remove the spell."

"I understand," Simon whispered, his eyes drifting closed. Gray tightened his hold on Simon's hand, and Simon squeezed back.

"Simon, I need you to center yourself. Isolate your magic as much as you can, do you understand?"

"Yes, sir." Simon took a deep breath, and Gray heard his heart rate speed up. Cormac met Gray's eyes, and Gray could see the puzzlement in the vampire's expression. Gray knew Simon's nervousness stemmed from the simple request for Simon to center himself. Gray looked away and brushed his thumb over Simon's knuckles.

"Easy, Simon. Remember what Garon said? Don't force it, just let it happen."

Simon smiled and let out his breath, and Gray could feel him settle. Cormac shot Gray another confused look, and Gray had a feeling he'd be answering a few more questions later.

"I'm ready, Grandfather."

"Very good." Cormac closed his eyes and held his hand over the stone. He grunted when Simon arched his back off the table and cried out. Gray used his free arm to hold Simon in place, and Liam went to his other side and added his hold to the mix.

"Come on, you bastard," Cormac yelled, sweat beginning to form on his head.

Simon screamed, and Gray nearly came undone. He began to shift and watched Liam's hands turn to claws beside his. They both growled as the scream continued. Finally Simon collapsed back against the table, and Cormac fell away, holding the stone tightly in his hand. "Gotcha," he whispered as his back hit the wall, and he slid down onto the floor.

17

Simon opened his eyes and blinked up at the ceiling. He could hear low growls beside him and turned to look at Gray. "It's gone," he smiled. He felt no presence of the darkness in his mind.

"Not gone," Cormac said from his place on the floor. He held up the stone, now streaked with red. "Trapped."

Simon tried to sit up and turn around so he could see. Gray helped him up, and Simon stared at Cormac. "Thank you."

"Now, why don't we see if we can track this thing to its source and put an end to this." Cormac pushed himself to his feet, and Liam reached out to grab his arm and steady him. "Thank you, wolf."

Liam grunted, and Simon couldn't stop a chuckle from escaping. "I feel really good," he said, then laughed again. Gray ran his hand down Simon's back, and Simon turned to meet his eyes. They shared a heated look, and Simon had to bite his lip to keep back a moan. Man, he felt really, really good.

"As you should." Cormac lifted a piece of purple velvet from the cabinet and wrapped the stone. "Whatever did this was strong, but the magic is growing weaker. We need to find it now, before it has a chance to do anything else."

Simon agreed. If they could find the demon and end this now, there was a chance he could actually have a leg to stand on with the Council. "I'm ready," he said and slid off the table. His legs wobbled, but Gray wrapped an arm around him and held him steady.

"You can find it using the stone?" Gray sounded disbelieving.

"I can," Cormac replied. "Just as you can find your wolves using your magic, I can find other soul magic users using mine. Especially if I hold a piece of their magic in my hand."

Simon watched as Cormac gathered a few things. He pushed up his sleeve and strapped on a leather band, then removed a second dagger from the wall. He slid it into the wrist sheath and made sure it was secure. Several crystals went from the cabinet into his pockets before he announced he was ready.

Gray and Liam still had their hands in partially shifted form, so they didn't require any weapons. Cormac eyed Simon and went back to the cabinet for another crystal. He wrapped this one in silver wire and put it around Simon's neck. He twisted the ends of the wire together to hold it in place.

"Keep that on, Simon, and remember that this demon is now attuned to your magic. It will be easier for it to attach itself to you a second time. This thing is desperate if it is doing these types of spells."

"I understand." Simon placed his hand over the necklace and felt an immediate sense of security. He gave it a gentle squeeze and offered silent thanks for its protection. He turned to Gray, half expecting Gray to protest his going along. Unlike the others, he would be unarmed, with just his magic to protect him. Gray didn't say a word, and Simon didn't mention the fact to him.

They left Cormac's house, the vampire replacing spells on each door as they passed through them. Simon wanted to learn how to do those spells, wanted to be able to protect himself and his home. He nearly stopped in his tracks when that thought didn't bring to mind his little cabin but Gray's house at the compound.

Gray drove again, but this time Cormac got the front seat. Simon and Liam sat in the back. Cormac gave directions to Gray, vague ones that were generally just a direction. "Go left," he said, then after a while, "now right."

Simon ignored them for the most part, concentrating more on his magic and how he was feeling. The leech had affected him more than he'd realized, especially now that it was gone and he was back to himself again. Each moment, he grew stronger, as if the magic he'd been using to keep the leech trapped in its little bubble was now being used to refill his nearly empty stores.

"DAMN it," Cormac said after they'd been driving a few minutes. "It's weakening faster than it should. You need to drive faster."

The car lurched as Gray slammed down on the gas.

"Keep going north. Hmm. Slightly east."

The SUV flew, and Simon held onto the handle of the door tightly as each turn threatened to send him flying across the seat.

"Fuck, we're heading straight for the compound." Gray's voice was angrier than Simon had ever heard it.

"Contact your pack, Alpha. Tell them to remain together. The demon will attack with no provocation at this point. It is dying and needs more magic quickly."

Simon felt Gray's magic, could actually hear him in his head for the first time. He warned the pack, gave instructions through the mind-link he shared with them. Liam nodded his agreement as each order was issued.

"Gray, what about the patrol? Should we leave them out?"

"No," Cormac interrupted. "They need to stay in a group. An isolated wolf or two will be at risk, even in its weakened state."

Gray sent yet another message even as he sped toward the compound.

A loud crack sounded, and Cormac jerked in his seat. "Damn it," he cursed again. "It's dead."

Simon leaned forward. The black stone lay in several pieces where it rested on the cloth in Cormac's hand. "What do we do now?"

"We keep going."

Gray didn't argue and kept the SUV at its high rate of speed. Several minutes passed before they reached the entrance to the compound. Gray and Liam both jumped out and shifted to their wolf forms before Simon even had his door open. They took off into the woods, howling into the darkness.

Simon could barely process what he'd just witnessed. He'd never seen Gray in wolf form—and really hadn't seen much more than a blur as they ran into the trees. Cormac got out, grabbed Simon's arm, and pulled him along.

"Come on, Simon. We need to find it."

Simon knew that, even if he had no idea what they were going to do when they found it. They followed the howls, running through the woods. Simon kept tripping over every stick and stone in his path. Branches slapped him in the face and his shirt kept getting caught as he tried to keep up.

"Cormac, go ahead. I know you can get there faster without me slowing you down."

Cormac seemed torn, but after a moment's hesitation, he picked up his pace and ran out of Simon's sight. Simon tried to keep running but had to slow down before he hurt himself. He yelped in fright when he felt fur brush against his side. He hadn't seen or heard the wolf approach.

It was pack, Simon could sense that much, even though he didn't know who exactly it was. It put its head under Simon's hand and bumped up. Simon grabbed hold of its soft fur and let the wolf lead him through the woods.

There was a slight break in the trees, not even big enough to be called a clearing. Simon could barely make out the shapes of wolves and men standing there. Gray and Liam were back in human form, their pale, bare skin easy to make out against the darkness.

Gray came to him and rubbed his hand over a small scratch on Simon's face. "You okay?"

Simon nodded, and Gray reached out to rub the wolf's head at his side absently. After a moment, Gray stepped aside, and Simon could see what he'd been shielding from view with his naked body.

The demon's corpse was sprawled in the brush, shriveled and shrunken. Simon recognized it, but it wasn't easy. There wasn't much left of the thing that had attacked him.

Cormac knelt at its side, his eyes closed in concentration. "It is completely drained."

"What does that mean?" Simon asked.

"That means that its magic is gone. All of it."

"I don't understand," Gray said.

Cormac rose to his feet. "I don't either. I'll need to take the body back to my home so I can try to glean more information from it. I don't like the looks of this at all."

Simon took a step closer. "Cormac, please. Tell me what this means. I thought it was over."

"It very well may be. This demon dealt in dark magics, and this may have been that magic backfiring on it. Or it could be something else. I just don't know yet. Alpha, could I trouble you for a ride back to my place?"

"No problem," Gray said. "Liam, give Cormac a ride back and assist him in any way he needs. Contact me if you learn anything."

"Yes, Alpha."

Cormac and Liam lifted the body and carried it back through the woods. Simon started to follow them, but Gray placed his hand on his shoulder, and Simon stopped. "I need to help."

"Simon, let him go. He knows this magic and you don't. Liam will contact me if they need help."

"But—"

"Please, Simon. Let's go see Garon and let him know we're okay."

The thought of Garon concerned about them, worried for their safety, was enough to convince Simon. "Okay."

"I'll shift and you hold on to me."

Simon nodded and the next thing he knew Gray was again a wolf. He noticed more this time, now that he was close and Gray wasn't running into the night. Before that first night, when he had seen the wolf at his car window, Simon hadn't known just how big the wolves were in shifted form.

He'd imagined the wolf more like a large dog, a lab or something. Gray was easily twice that size. His back reached Simon's waist and his head was nearly at Simon's chest. Gray looked up at him, and even in the darkness, Simon could see his eyes were the same.

Simon ran his hand over Gray's head, behind his ears. Gray pushed into him, nearly knocking him over. Simon laughed and did it again before grabbing a handful of fur and letting Gray lead him through the woods.

The rest of the wolves followed them, one after the other stepping up to Simon's free side and pressing their heads into his hand. He rubbed each of them in return. It comforted him, knowing they were there beside and behind him, watching over him as Gray led him home.

A break appeared in the trees up ahead, and moments later they were on the drive leading into the compound. Gray shifted again, his naked body magically appearing where the wolf had stood moments before.

His power intoxicated Simon, aroused him in a way Simon didn't really understand. All he knew was he wanted more. Gray had barely missed a step during the change, but Simon found himself stumbling more than ever, though they were on even ground. His gaze was stuck on Gray, fascinated in turn by the beauty of his long legs and the powerful muscles of his chest. He couldn't seem to concentrate on where he was walking.

Gray steadied him after the second stumble and looked at him with concern. What he saw in Simon's eyes made him catch his breath and then smirk at Simon knowingly. He threw his arm around Simon's shoulders and pulled him close.

Simon wound his arm around Gray's waist, his bare skin hot to the touch. He traced his fingers over Gray's ribs, down to the slight indention of his side, and then back up again. Simon's steps became surer now that he was keeping pace with Gray.

The cabins of the pack began to appear as they got closer to the center of the compound, and Gray hurried them along. The wolves following them drifted away one by one, breaking off to go back to their own homes. After a few minutes, Gray and Simon were alone and walking the final steps to the main house.

When they reached a particularly dark spot under a huge oak in the yard, Gray spun Simon around and pulled him close. "Fuck, what you do to me." He devoured Simon's lips with his, and Simon opened to him without hesitation.

He'd never wanted this much, needed this much. He gripped Gray's muscled back, pulling him closer and closer until there was nothing between them but the thin material of Simon's clothes. He longed to rip his shirt off and throw it aside, leaving only their skin touching.

Gray broke away, gasping for breath, his cock hard against Simon's stomach. "I want you," he whispered, his voice hoarse and raspy.

"Yes, please," Simon said, before pulling Gray close again.

Gray held him back, chuckling. "We have to wait. Just a few more minutes."

Simon groaned, but he knew Garon was waiting for them inside, just a few steps away. "You can't go in like that." Simon gestured to Gray's straining erection.

"I know." Gray sighed, and Simon felt the tingle of his magic. A minute later the front door opened, and Aunt Maggie tossed something out into the yard. Gray went over and picked up the pair of shorts and slipped them on. His cock was still slightly obscene, outlined clearly against the thin fabric. "Just stay kind of in front of me for a minute."

Simon laughed and nodded. They went onto the porch and in through the front door. Garon came barreling through the living room at them and grabbed Simon in a hug.

"Did you get it out?"

Simon nodded. "Yep. It's gone."

"I heard Dad say it was here, but everything's okay now, right?"

Gray spoke up behind him. "Everything's fine, kiddo. No one is hurt, and the demon is dead."

"Oh. Did you have to kill it, Dad?"

"No, it was dead when we found it. Nothing to worry about, though. We're taking care of it, okay?"

"Okay. You're sure it's dead?"

Gray slipped around a bit so he could wrap himself around both Garon and Simon. "I'm sure, son."

Garon breathed a sigh of relief. "I know it's not okay to be glad someone died, but I kind of am."

Simon gave him a little squeeze. "It's okay, Garon. I have to say I'm a little bit glad myself. The demon was dangerous and trying to hurt us. I wish it didn't have to end that way, but I'd rather it die than one of us, you know?"

"Yeah. I was pretty scared."

Simon looked up into Gray's eyes. "Yeah, I was too. But we don't have to worry. Your dad will keep us safe."

18

*G*ray and Simon helped Garon get settled into bed. Gray wasn't sure who needed the ritual more, his son or himself. They tucked him in, and Gray ran his hand over Garon's hair for a few minutes. Garon pushed into the touch and reached out his other hand to grab Simon's. After a few moments, Gray leaned down and kissed his son's forehead. Simon gave Garon's fingers a gentle squeeze before releasing them and stepping back. Garon slipped easily into sleep.

As Gray led Simon out of the room and into the hall, his gaze drifted across the hall to the guest room where Simon's things were, and then down the hall to the master bedroom. He knew where he wanted them to end up. Glancing at Simon, he could see Simon was having similar thoughts. "Stay with me tonight?"

Simon's eyes grew dark with lust. "I'd love to."

They went slowly down the hall, hands locked together. Gray led Simon into his room and pulled him over to the bed. He turned on a small lamp on the bedside table, its soft glow providing just enough light for them to maneuver. Gray guided Simon around so he was sitting on the bed before he knelt down to slip off Simon's shoes. He tossed them aside, followed by his socks.

Simon started to unfasten his jeans, but Gray brushed his hands away. "Let me."

Simon nodded and leaned back so Gray had easier access to the front of his jeans. He bit his lip, suddenly anxious. "I should probably shower."

"Later," Gray whispered.

He trailed his hands up Simon's long legs, brushing his fingers against the roughness of the denim. Finally reaching Simon's waist, he unsnapped then unzipped the fastenings before guiding the stubborn fabric down Simon's hips. Simon lifted his body slightly and allowed Gray to pull them over the muscles of his ass and down his legs.

Gray threw the jeans over his shoulder, and they joined the growing pile of clothing on the floor. He worked his way back down Simon's legs, this time trailing his hands over Simon's lightly haired skin. Simon threw his head back and bit his lip.

The slightest touch between them was enough to set Simon's pulse racing. Gray lifted Simon's left leg and trailed kisses all the way to his thigh. He bit gently at the sensitive skin there, and Simon groaned beneath him.

"Gray… please."

"Shh. I've got you." He lowered Simon's left leg and lifted his right, repeating the process. When he reached Simon's thigh again, he nuzzled under the leg of his boxer briefs and pushed the material up to get a taste of the skin hidden under them.

Simon spread his legs wider as Gray kissed his way over the boxers and up to Simon's stomach, pushing his T-shirt up inch by inch as he went.

"Damn, I love your body," Gray said against Simon's ribs, his breath heating the skin. He licked his way up farther, to a pink nipple that begged to be tasted.

Gray tugged at the tight bud with his teeth, and Simon hissed and arched beneath him. He grabbed Gray's head and held it in place as Gray continued to tease him. Gray moved to the other side, licked the second little nub, then blew gently on it as it pebbled and hardened with the stimulation.

Simon grabbed the hem of his T-shirt and pulled it off. He threw it aside and slid his hand back to Gray's head and guided him up farther, to his neck. Gray explored the tender skin there and kissed the spot that made Simon gasp and plead for more before he finally made his way to Simon's mouth.

The kiss wasn't long enough. Simon groaned when Gray pulled away from him to kneel on the bed between Simon's spread legs. Simon slid himself farther onto the mattress, and Gray stretched out over him. Their lips met again, and Simon delved his tongue deeply into Gray's mouth. Gray continued to explore, his large hand cupping Simon's heavy balls and hard cock where they remained hidden beneath his briefs.

"Gray, please. Don't tease me anymore. I can't wait."

"We have all night."

Simon laughed against his mouth. "*You* might have all night. I have about thirty seconds until I explode."

"I can work with that." Gray gave him that familiar smirk and pushed the elastic of Simon's black boxer briefs over his stiff length. He pulled and tugged to get them off. Simon helped to kick the material off his legs and out of the way.

When Simon was free, Gray turned around so his head was at Simon's groin, and positioned his hips near Simon's head, in case he wanted to explore as well. He wanted another close-up look at Simon's dick as it strained for his touch. He gave it a quick lick, then sucked the tip into his mouth. Simon groaned and began to fumble with the elastic of Gray's shorts, tugging them down just far enough to free Gray's cock.

As Gray sucked Simon deeper into his mouth, he traced the veined base with his hand. Simon returned the favor, licking at Gray before he sucked him in deep. Gray groaned around Simon's dick, the sensations on his own warring with the pleasure he was getting from tasting Simon.

His groan made Simon arch and thrust into him. Gray swallowed quickly, trying not to choke on his sudden mouthful. Simon let go of Gray's cock long enough to mumble, "Sorry," then went right back to it. Their motions fed off each other. Gray sucked and stroked, slowly at first, savoring the taste, and Simon matched his rhythm.

When Gray needed harder and faster, he pulled Simon's dick deep into his mouth. Simon was heat and sweat and man... and blackberries. Gray bobbed a bit too hard over that realization and nearly choked himself again. He pulled off with a grin. "You taste really good."

"Hmm," Simon moaned.

Gray got a firm grip on Simon's dick and stroked. "Like blackberries."

Simon paused and looked down his body, then pulled his mouth off Gray. "My soap. Blackberry and sage."

Gray nuzzled Simon's sac, licking his lightly furred balls. "I like it."

Simon groaned and stroked Gray in a tight fist. "I'm glad."

Gray sucked a finger into his mouth and had it dripping with saliva before going on a quest for Simon's hole. The first touch of his finger against Simon's pucker made Simon arch and squeeze his ass together. "Oh fuck."

"Yeah," Gray grinned, licking his lips. "That's what I want. Relax for me, baby." When Simon unclenched his body, Gray dipped his finger into Simon's body, just the tip breaching him. Simon let go of Gray's cock and gripped his leg and the sheets.

"Deeper," Simon demanded.

Gray pushed his finger in farther, feeling Simon's tight hole stretch around him. He pulled out and dripped a little more spit onto his finger before pushing it in again. "You like that?"

"Yes, God, yes. More."

Gray slipped his hand free, then knelt up and reached over to the nightstand and dug around until he found his lube. He drizzled some over his fingers, then pushed two slowly inside Simon's body. He rolled them around inside, making sure he got Simon nice and slick. When the muscles loosened, he crooked his fingers up to brush over that little nub inside.

Simon arched his back and moaned, reaching for his cock to give it a quick stroke. Gray used his other hand to knock Simon's away. "Leave that alone."

Simon glared down at him but dropped his head back when Gray nudged his prostate again. Seeing Simon's intense reactions to him made Gray harder than he'd thought possible. He stilled his fingers inside Simon as he rearranged his body, twisting and turning until he was positioned where he wanted to be, between Simon's legs.

"You ready, baby?"

"Yes. Now, Gray."

Sliding his fingers free, Gray added a bit more lube over his cock and placed it at the opening of Simon's body. A gentle push and the crown breached Simon, the muscles stretching farther to allow Gray's thick length access. They both groaned, Simon's legs coming up to open himself wider.

"Yes," he panted. "Do it."

Gray leaned forward, bracing his body on his hands on either side of Simon. He started thrusting carefully, going just a bit deeper with each push of his hips. Simon grabbed Gray's arms and arched his body upward, helping Gray glide farther and farther inside his body until at last their hips met and Gray was completely sheathed inside him.

Lowering himself to his elbows, Gray tried not to crush Simon beneath his weight. Simon lifted his head and met Gray's lips as they moved together and found their rhythm. He wrapped his raised legs around Gray's waist, allowing Gray's cock to go as deep as it could. He clutched at Gray's shoulders, digging his fingers into the flexing muscles.

Gray wanted it to go on forever, but the wait had been too long, and feeling Simon's tight heat, clenching and releasing, his arms and legs grasping and frantically searching for purchase, pushed Gray over the edge. He buried his head in Simon's neck, holding back the howl that threatened to emerge as he came in thick, hot spurts inside Simon's body.

Simon quickly followed, the final, hard thrusts from Gray hitting him just right and forcing his own climax. They gasped together, Gray thrusting lazily as Simon continued to jerk beneath him. When they subsided, Gray let more of his weight rest on Simon, their hot breath mingling as they nuzzled each other's faces.

"Fuck, Simon. That was incredible."

Simon chuckled and nudged him to the side. "Yeah."

"Oh, here we go again. You can't talk after, can you?"

"Nope."

Gray slid his cock from Simon's hole, and he could feel the wetness slipping free with it. He grabbed some tissues from the night-stand and helped Simon clean up before wiping himself off as well.

Simon just lay there with a goofy grin, tracing one hand over the hard planes of Gray's chest. Gray settled back beside him and curled onto his side so he could tuck Simon close. Simon rolled over slightly so they were facing each other and snuggled in next to Gray. He sighed and wrapped an arm around Gray's waist. "Sleepy," he mumbled.

Gray was energized after sex and wanted nothing more than to rest a minute and go again. Simon wouldn't be up for it that soon, though, and he ran his hand softly down Simon's side. "Rest. I'm not going anywhere."

Simon nodded and his eyes drifted shut. A minute later his breathing deepened as he fell asleep. Gray lay next to him, continuing the soft strokes down Simon's side. He rested his head on his other hand so he could stare down at Simon and watch him as he sank further into dreamland.

19

Simon woke up wrapped in the warmth of Gray's body beneath him. He was sprawled half over Gray's chest, their legs tangled together and Gray's arms firm around him. He pried open one eye and glared at the alarm clock. Six thirty. His internal clock never failed him, no matter how much he wanted it to.

His bladder also insisted it was time to get up, so he tried to untangle himself from Gray's hold. Gray grumbled and pulled him back. Simon poked him in the side, and Gray opened his eyes with a scowl. "What?"

"I have to pee. Let me get up."

Gray grunted his disapproval but moved his arms and let Simon climb out of bed. His ass ached, but in that good, well-fucked way that reminded him how good Gray had felt inside him the night before. He did his business and caught a whiff of himself. A shower was the first thing on his to-do list for the day.

He went back to the bedroom and found Gray curled up around a pillow, so he slipped into his jeans and went into the guest room. After gathering up a change of clothes and his herbal soap, Simon retreated to the hall bathroom for a nice, long shower.

When he came out, he could smell breakfast cooking downstairs and made his way to the kitchen. Aunt Maggie was at the stove, making a big pot of something that smelled spectacular. "Well, good morning! You're up early."

"The early bird gets first dibs on breakfast," Simon said with a grin.

"That he does. Here, try this." She held out her wooden spoon, which was covered in a thick, white sauce. Simon blew on it to cool it down, then took a small taste.

"Mmm. That's good. What is it?"

"Goldenrod eggs."

"Never had that."

"Oh, it's just boiled eggs chopped up in a white sauce. Sounds fancy, but it's not. Garon likes them because he can crumble the yolk over the top."

"Doesn't he sleep in on the weekends?"

"That boy doesn't know the meaning of the word. I'm surprised he isn't down here already. The sun comes up, and he's out of bed." About that time, they heard a door open upstairs and then the bathroom door in the hall close. "And there he is," Aunt Maggie said with a little chuckle.

"I'm like that as well. Up at six thirty, whether I want to be or not. It's annoying sometimes."

Garon came into the kitchen, rubbing his eyes, as Simon finished speaking. His hair was sticking up all over the place, and his shirt was half-tucked into his pajama pants. He walked over to Simon and leaned against him, blinking sleepily. "Morning," Simon said, wrapping an arm over Garon's shoulders for a brief hug.

Aunt Maggie grinned over her shoulder at them. "He might get up early, but he doesn't talk for a few. He's like his daddy that way. And speaking of, I'd better get the coffee on. Pre-coffee Gray is not pleasant."

Garon giggled into Simon's side. "Dad says coffee is his go-juice."

Simon laughed, thinking of how talkative Gray liked to be at other times. It was good to know he was grumbly sometimes too. "Well, my go-juice is a morning meditation, which I'd better get to if I want to eat breakfast while it's still hot. Do I have time?"

"Oh, sure. The sauce needs to thicken up a bit more. Will ten minutes or so do you?"

"Yep, that'll work. Just holler out the back door if I'm not in when it's ready."

"Will do."

"Hey, Simon, can I come with you?"

Simon stared over at him in surprise. "Well, sure, if you want to. You'll have to be quiet though, okay?"

Garon grinned. "I can be quiet. Sometimes."

Aunt Maggie snorted, and they all laughed as Simon and Garon went out the back door. Once they reached the grass, Simon sat down and crossed his legs. Garon mirrored his movements, and they sat facing each other in the early morning light.

"Now, what I do is just sit quietly for a minute and concentrate on settling my magic for the day. Just a little pick-me-up to make sure everything is how I want it. You want to try?"

"Sure!" Garon closed his eyes and put his hands on his knees. Simon smiled and did the same. He focused his energy and was amazed at how quickly he became centered. It was effortless—which it hadn't been for a very long time.

After a few minutes of meditation, Simon peeked through one eye to see what Garon was doing. He had to bite his lip to keep from laughing. Garon was sitting in the same position, but his head was bobbing as he kept falling asleep and jerking awake, only to fall asleep again.

Simon took pity on him, still chuckling to himself, and gently shook Garon's shoulder. His eyes darted open, and he yawned widely. "Sorry, Simon."

Simon stood up and pulled Garon up as well. "No problem. Sometimes that happens." They went back into the kitchen to find Aunt Maggie plating up breakfast and Gray blinking and scowling over a cup of coffee at the table. Garon went over and leaned against him, and they rubbed their heads together for a moment before Garon sat down beside him.

"Where were you guys?" Gray's voice was still low and scratchy from sleep, and he seemed especially grumpy.

"We meditated, Dad! Well, Simon meditated. I kinda fell asleep." Garon's little nap in the yard seemed to have energized him. Gray looked back and forth at them, then glared back down at his coffee. He took a small sip and leaned back in his chair with a quiet sigh.

Aunt Maggie placed plates in front of Garon and Simon. Garon took the little ball of yolk from the side and crumbled it over his food with glee. Simon attempted to copy him, but he ended up with a mess of yolk all over his fingers. After cleaning himself off on his napkin, Simon gave the mysterious-looking egg concoction a taste. "Wow. This is really good."

Garon grinned around his mouthful. "I know," he said, and dug back in.

Gray arched a brow at him. "Manners," he said.

Garon chewed and swallowed before answering. "Sorry. But it is really good."

"Thanks, sweetie," Aunt Maggie said.

"What are we going to do today, Dad?"

Gray shrugged and took another drink of his coffee.

"I think we should show Simon around. Wouldn't that be cool? He hasn't seen anything here yet. We could show him the meeting hall, and maybe go see the other kids, oh, and we could go swimming at the pond!"

Gray looked at Simon, who was busily eating his breakfast. "That sounds like fun to me. Simon?"

Simon hadn't really thought about what he wanted to do. He should probably pack up and head back to his place, but the idea of spending the day with them was too tempting to resist. "I think that sounds awesome."

"Yes!" Garon yelled. Gray winced and drank more coffee. Simon just grinned and enjoyed a morning that wasn't him eating a piece of toast by himself.

It took about an hour for them to finish breakfast, do the morning cleanup, and head out for their tour. Garon guided them, knowing the history of the property very well. The pack was founded in the early 1900s, the result of a division of a larger pack over the mountains around Asheville. The earliest High Moon Pack members had pooled their money and purchased the property that the pack still held today.

Garon took them to an old cabin set away from the rest. "Simon, you have to be respectful here. This is our first Alpha's cabin." Garon was very serious, and Gray had to turn his head to keep his son from seeing his smile.

Simon looked into the small, one-room cabin as Garon watched to make sure he appreciated it. After making appropriate comments on its coolness, Garon led Simon back to the largest structure on the property. "This is really great. It was built in... Um, I don't remember, Dad?"

"1928," Gray supplied.

"Yeah, in 1928," Garon agreed. "The pack wanted a big meeting hall like the one they had in the other pack, so they started building one. But they were smart, weren't they, Dad?"

Gray nodded his agreement.

"They made it really big, big enough for a pack three times their size, because they knew we'd be a bigger, stronger pack one day."

"And they were right, weren't they?" Simon added.

"Yep. We're really big and strong now. Come on, Simon. I want to show you the cool part."

There were about twenty steps leading up to a large covered porch. Rocking chairs and benches were scattered around the planked floor, and a couple of ceiling fans whirled slowly, keeping the porch cool. Garon didn't stop to let Simon admire the sweeping view. Instead, he dragged Simon inside and over to a wall of photos displayed on the main wall.

Most were black and white and set on the porch of the meeting hall. Simon could see the distinctive gray hair in the patriarch of each picture, tracing down the line until they reached the end, where a color photo of Gray and a much younger Garon hung.

"Check it out, Simon. That's me and Dad. And in twenty years, I'll have my own picture to put right here beside it."

"Twenty years?" Simon asked.

"Yep. I get to be alpha when I turn thirty, just like Dad."

The history and tradition amazed Simon. He had nothing like this to pass down to the children he probably wouldn't have anyway. His legacy consisted of his cabin and his grandfather's journals. He couldn't trace his family back several generations, and now that he'd met Cormac and read about the death of his werewolf mate, Simon suddenly realized he might know why.

Gray put his arm discreetly around Simon's waist. "You okay?"

"Yeah. This is amazing, Gray."

Gray glanced around the room with quiet pride. "I think so. I used to think of all the things I'd change when I became alpha, all the things I'd make bigger and better." His gaze landed on the photo of him and Garon. "Now I think of all the ways I can keep it the same. What I can pass on to my son."

Simon stared up at him, suddenly longing to be part of those traditions, that history. He wondered if it would ever be possible for his photo to be there on the wall, right alongside Gray and Garon. The three of them, together as a family. His heart sped up, the quick rush of happiness at the idea surprising him.

SIMON was pleasantly exhausted after an afternoon of swimming and playing at the pond with Gray, Garon, and several other members of the pack. The three of them walked back to Gray's house to prepare for the impromptu cookout they had planned for the evening. Gray asked Aunt Maggie to defrost some hamburger meat so he could make his "famous" burgers on the grill. The other pack members they'd invited were bringing chips, potato salad, and baked beans.

Gray spoke to Liam midafternoon and learned Cormac hadn't made very much progress on the demon's corpse. Since its magic was completely drained, there wasn't much to work with. They were all frustrated but hoped the demon's death would mean the end of their troubles.

In the mood to celebrate, Gray told Liam to head back to the compound and join them for dinner. He invited Cormac as well, and Simon knew Gray hoped spending time with the vampire would ease Simon's worries a bit.

Simon did want to get to know the vampire more, but he wasn't quite as hopeful about the rest of his worries. He didn't remind Gray, not wanting to ruin their wonderful day, but he knew he still had to face the Conclave of Mages. It weighed heavily on him, even though Cormac didn't seem to believe he would get more than a slap on the wrist.

While doing his job of filling a cooler with ice, soda, and water, he kept one ear on the conversation going on in the kitchen between Gray and Garon. He didn't really want to eavesdrop, but Garon was grilling Gray about their relationship, and Simon found it incredibly amusing.

"So, do you kiss him and stuff?" Garon asked.

"Well, yeah," Gray answered.

"Hmm. I guess that's okay. He is pretty cool. Did you see him when we were playing chicken at the pond? We didn't even get dunked once!" Garon and Simon had been teamed up for the challenge. Garon, on Simon's shoulders, had tried to knock the other kids off their parents' shoulders and into the water. They were drenched multiple times but managed to stay on their feet.

"I saw him. You guys did great."

"Yeah. So, is he gonna stay here now and, I don't know, be your mate?"

"Kiddo, it's a little soon for us to be thinking about that, don't you think? Let's just hang out with Simon and be his friend, and we'll see what happens. The rest is grown-up stuff between me and Simon."

Garon sighed. "Well, I want him to stay, and I don't care if you kiss him or anything. It would be cool for you to have a mate like Mom and my friends' parents."

"Yeah, buddy, that would be cool."

Simon decided it was time to rescue Gray and went back into the kitchen. "My work here is done," he announced. "Can we eat yet?"

Garon snickered and held up a handful of raw hamburger. "Sure," he said with a giggle, "here you go."

"Blech. That looks gross."

"Yeah, it has anchovies."

"What?"

Gray laughed and pointed to the bottle of Worcestershire sauce. "It has anchovies in it."

"Oh, well, that's not so bad then." Simon took the bottle from Gray and read the ingredients. "You know, Garon, we could probably come up with some sort of secret recipe of our own using my herbs. What do you think?"

"Cool! Can Dad help?"

"Sure, if he wants to."

Gray met Simon's eyes, and they shared a secret smile.

"Yeah, he wants to," Gray murmured, and Simon knew he wasn't talking about herbs.

"Ugh," Garon complained. "You guys are acting like girls. Are you gonna kiss now?"

"Yes," Gray said and ran around the counter to grab Simon. He dipped him backward and placed a loud, smacking kiss on his forehead. When he stood Simon upright, he turned to Garon and wiggled his eyebrows. "You're next."

Simon and Gray both rounded the counter slowly, stalking Garon as he squealed and tried to get away without making a mess of the hamburger patties. "That's not fair! If I make a mess, Aunt Maggie will make me clean it up!"

"You should have thought of that," Gray said as he scooped Garon up in his arms. "You're mine now. Mwa-ha-ha!" He placed kisses all over Garon's head as Garon laughed and struggled to get away. Simon grabbed him from the other side, making a Garon sandwich, and they both kissed and tickled him until he was breathless.

After they put him down, Garon made faces at them and washed his hands. Simon cleaned up the little bit of mess on the floor. He felt a tingle of magic and looked up at Gray, who seemed to be listening to someone through his mind-link.

20

S imon held his breath, his anxiety spiking at the expression on Gray's face. Gray looked down at him and frowned when he saw Simon kneeling on the floor.

"Calm down, baby. It's just the guards letting me know Cormac and Liam are here."

Simon blew out a huff of air, and Gray pulled him to his feet.

"Everything is going to be okay, Simon."

"I hope so."

"It will be. Now let's go greet Grandpa Cormac." They left the kitchen and went through the living room to the front door. "Do you think he'll let you call him Papa? What about Pee Paw?" Gray's teasing worked, and Simon burst out laughing.

"You can call him that. I'm not going to."

"Oh, come on! I double-dog dare you."

"No way."

Gray pulled Simon against him and slid his hands down Simon's back and over his ass. "I bet I can think of something you want, some way to convince you."

"Uh-huh. Sure. You just keep thinking that."

They leaned together and shared a brief kiss before Garon called out from the kitchen. "Dad, I finished the burgers."

"Okay. I'll be back in a minute, and we'll get them on the grill."

"Hurry, Dad! I'm starving!"

Gray and Simon both laughed as Gray opened the door and they stepped out onto the front porch. Dusk gave the trees lengthy shadows, and night was fast approaching. Gray reached back inside and flipped the switch for the front porch light just as Liam's SUV pulled to a stop in front of the house.

There was palpable tension in the air as the pair got out of the vehicle. Liam barely glanced at Gray, only looking at him long enough to give him a quick nod before he went around back to the deck. Cormac glanced around the compound as he made his way up to the porch. "Lovely," he said, giving Gray a small smile.

"Thank you. It's been in our pack for several generations."

"I take it I am the first vampire to be welcome at the property?"

Gray shrugged a bit. "Sorry the guards weren't more welcoming. I'm sure you understand their tension right now."

"I do. I appreciate the invitation." Cormac looked over at Simon, who was watching the exchange silently.

"Hello, Simon."

Simon held out his hand, and Cormac shook it. Their hands remained joined for a long moment, then Cormac stepped closer and gave Simon a quick hug. "I can feel your anxiety, Simon. It's rolling off you in waves."

"Yeah," Simon replied. "I have a lot on my mind."

Gray ran his hand down Simon's back. "Will you be okay if I go start the burgers?"

"Yeah. I'll be fine."

"Okay. I'll just be around back if you need me. You guys can talk a bit."

As Gray walked away, Simon took the opportunity to study Cormac. He didn't know how far apart they were generation-wise or how old Cormac really was, but he wanted to see some small bit of himself in his ancestor.

Ancestor. It was odd to think of him that way. Cormac didn't seem old, didn't appear much over thirty. He really didn't even much look like a vampire, or at least what Simon thought a vampire should look like. The ones on television and in the movies always seemed to be wearing leather and flowing capes. Cormac wore dark jeans and a white button-down shirt. Nothing fancy or flashy and no "creature of the night" vibe.

Simon thought maybe they should at least look alike or something, but their looks weren't similar either. Where Simon's hair was dark brown and straight, Cormac's was much lighter and had a bit of curl to it. Cormac was shorter than Simon, but maybe their noses were sort of the same. At least it was something.

An old swing hung at one end of the porch, and Simon led Cormac to it. They sat down, and Simon set it in gentle motion with one foot. Now that he had Cormac here, Simon didn't have any idea what to say.

Fortunately, Cormac broke the ice. "It was very thoughtful of Gray to invite me. Especially considering the circumstances."

"Yeah. He doesn't want the pack to freak out over every Other they come across, you know?"

"Understandable."

"And I think he knew I wanted to get to know you better."

"I would like that, Simon. It's been difficult staying away these past years, but I needed to respect your grandfather's wishes. He loved you very much."

Simon nodded. "He was the only one, you know? The one who understood and could help me get through things. It really sucked that I only had him for a few years after we found out I would be a mage."

"Yes, it did. It was a great loss. He was an amazing man."

"Did you ever think about turning him? I mean, you could have, couldn't you?"

Cormac shook his head. "It wasn't what he wanted. He'd known for years that he had a heart defect and that his time would be limited. I offered several times, but he was wise and knew it wasn't his path."

"Yeah."

"I know he wouldn't have wanted to leave you. Oh, how he would go on about you. Every little thing made him so proud. When the mage ability skipped your father, we both thought our line would end with him."

Simon gave the swing another push to keep it moving. "He told me about that once. When he explained that he was giving me the cabin and leaving me money. It really pissed my dad off."

"He did it to protect you, you know that, right?"

"I guess I never thought about it."

Cormac turned slightly so he was facing Simon. "Simon, I know you don't know me well, but I will protect you as well. You're my family, the last of my line. I will do anything I can to keep you safe."

Simon turned his head to keep Cormac from seeing his expression. "All I've ever wanted was a real family. Since Granddad passed, I've been so alone."

"You've never been alone, Simon." Cormac put his foot down and stopped the swing. He grabbed Simon's chin gently and turned him so they faced each other. "Even when you didn't know I was there, I watched over you."

Simon smiled and reached up to hold on to Cormac's hand where it rested on his face. "Thank you."

"We're going to get through all this together. I don't know what's going on with you and the alpha, but I want you to know you're welcome to come stay with me for a while. Now that I'm able, I want to know you better. I see a lot of myself in you."

Simon chuckled. "Is that a good thing?"

Cormac chucked him under the chin and laughed. "Of course. Don't you know I'm amazing?"

"Oh sure. I had to get it from somewhere, didn't I?"

Cormac shook his head and smiled. They both turned on the swing and faced the yard again. Cormac pushed it back into motion, and they gently rocked back and forth for a few moments.

"I see what you like about this place. It is very comforting."

"It is."

"And I'm sure having that big hunk of a wolf around doesn't hurt anything, does it?"

Simon blushed and shook his head. "No, that doesn't hurt at all. Well, maybe in a good way." Simon laughed and covered his mouth at his audacity.

Cormac joined him. "You know that you get the attraction to wolves from me, don't you? It must run in the family."

Simon was surprised Cormac brought up his familiar, but he did so with a smile, so Simon just nodded and continued swinging.

"My Silas was a gray wolf, just like your pack here. He was a handsome devil, too. Swept me right off my feet. It wasn't done in those days, you know?"

Simon nodded his agreement. He couldn't imagine what it must have been like for them so long ago, with all the troubles their kind still faced.

"Still, I knew he was meant for me the moment I saw him. We mages are so solitary that it surprised me. So many years, and I still miss him."

Simon reached over and grabbed Cormac's hand and gave it a squeeze. Cormac let out a long breath and shook his head. "Enough of the trip down memory lane."

"I don't mind," Simon said. "It's nice to know the history. He's part of my family too."

"Thank you, Simon. Now, let's go find that wolf of yours and get some dinner. I do believe your stomach would appreciate it."

Simon rubbed his stomach as it let out a loud grumble. "I think you're right. Hey, can you eat? Because I've heard Gray's burgers are amazing."

They stood up and made their way around the house. "Yes, I can eat. I function as a human does for the most part. I just occasionally need blood for my magic to remain stable."

Several pack members were gathered on the deck. They watched Cormac as he and Simon approached. None of them seemed open to his presence. Garon, on the other hand, had no fear. He ran right up to Simon and tugged on his arm. "Simon, come on. Dad's almost done with the burgers, and I want you to sit with me. You can sit with us too, uh... I forgot your name."

"Cormac."

"Cool. Cormac." Garon got between them and pulled them both toward a long folding table set up on the deck. "Are you really a vampire? 'Cause I've never met a vampire or anything, but you don't really look like a vampire."

"Yes, I'm really a vampire."

"Hmm." Garon stared up at him a moment. "So you aren't going to like, suck my blood or anything gross, right?"

"Of course not."

"'Kay." That seemed to be all the reassurance Garon needed, and he began chattering in his usual way.

Gray took the burgers off the grill and placed them on a large platter. He set it in the center of the table, and everyone's attention turned to him. Simon thought they were expecting some sort of speech or explanation, but Gray simply smiled. "Let's eat."

When everyone's plates were loaded up, Simon looked around the deck and thought about how much his life had changed. There was an old expression his grandfather used to say. Something about when a door closed, a window opened. It was definitely a good description of his life recently.

They were just finishing up when Simon felt Gray's magic, and everyone turned to him. His face tensed, and he looked at Simon. "There are mages at the gate. They want to speak to you."

Simon's heart rate sped up. Gray wrapped an arm around him and was joined by Garon on Simon's other side. "What do they want, Simon?" Garon asked.

"I don't know, but I guess it would be rude to keep them waiting. I'll go meet them at the gate," Simon said. Gray didn't want them on the property any more than he did, and Simon wouldn't let them get any closer if he could help it.

"I'll go with you," Gray said.

"Me too," Garon added.

Simon knelt down in front of him. "Listen, Gar, I know you want to come too, but I think it would be better if you waited here." He stopped Garon before he could protest. "It's not that I don't want you with me, but here's the thing. They don't know that you can do mage magic, and I think it's better if we keep that a secret for now."

Garon sniffed and hugged Simon. "I don't want you to go."

"Hey," he whispered into Garon's hair, "I'm sure they just need to talk to me. Don't worry, okay?"

"You'll come back?"

"I will do my best, but I might have to go with them tonight."

Gray placed a hand on Garon's shoulder and squeezed gently, trying to comfort him as best he could. Gray obviously hated seeing his son so upset, but bottom line, they had to keep Garon protected, and they weren't sure this scene wouldn't turn out to be a fight. Simon knew Gray wasn't just going to hand him over to the mages.

Cormac stood beside them, ready to stand by Simon. Simon placed a hand on his shoulder and squeezed. "Same for you, Cormac. I think we should keep you a secret a bit longer. I don't want to add more fuel to the fire, you know?"

Simon knew Cormac didn't want to be left out and that he wanted to stand by Simon. It just wasn't the right time, and Cormac agreed to stay behind.

21

*G*ray drove his SUV down to the gate, and Simon seemed surprised to see several other pack members standing there as well. He looked at the growing crowd and, puzzled, turned to Gray. "What are they all doing here?"

Gray grabbed his hand and squeezed. "They're here for you."

"Did you tell them to come?"

"No." And he hadn't, although Gray admitted to himself he would have if he had thought of it.

"Okay, let's do this." Simon got out and went over to the gate. A blond man stepped forward, and Simon bowed his head slightly in acknowledgment.

Gray growled under his breath at the gesture, the wolf in him pissed at seeing Simon submit to anyone else. The man in him wasn't very happy about it either. He forced himself to calm down when Simon glanced over at him in concern.

"Hello, Master Thomas," Simon said when he was convinced Gray was okay.

"Simon, I must say I'm disturbed at finding you here."

Gray stared at Thomas, this supposed master of Simon's who had tossed him aside when Simon needed guidance the most. He moved closer to Simon's side, wanting nothing more than to challenge the man where he stood.

Simon didn't acknowledge the censure in the mage's voice, and Gray was relieved. "What can I do for you, Master Thomas? We were in the middle of dinner."

Several of the wolves grumbled their displeasure, and Master Thomas glared around at them before returning his attention to Simon. "The Conclave requires your presence for a special hearing on your circumstances."

Simon paused for a moment, looked around at the pack and then back at the mages. He reached over, took Gray's hand, and laced their fingers together. "I'd be happy to set up a time to speak with them."

Gray nearly howled his pleasure. Simon belonged with them, and it appeared he was willing to make his stand.

"They want you now, Simon."

Feeling Simon's hesitation, Gray spoke up. "Like he said, we're in the middle of dinner. We'd be happy to set up a meeting on neutral grounds to discuss matters."

Thomas laughed, and the sound chilled Gray. Simon shivered beside him. "Oh, Alpha, I know you think you're in charge here, but I hate to tell you that you aren't. Simon can certainly choose to remain here, and if he does, he will force the Conclave to come get him." His eyes turned to Simon. "Is that really what you want to happen?"

The threat was clear. Gray and the rest of the pack tensed, ready for whatever the mages planned to do next. Simon looked around at them all and shook his head. "No, that's not what I want." He slipped his hand from Gray's and turned to him. "I won't put the pack at risk."

"Simon, you don't have to do this. My earlier option is still on the table." Gray didn't want to fight, didn't want some big battle on his hands, but he couldn't let Simon just walk away.

"I know. And when I get back, I want to talk to you about that."

Master Thomas smiled triumphantly. "Come along, Simon."

Gray growled at him, and his smile fell as he stepped back. "Know this, mage, if you harm one hair on his head, the fury of this pack will be on you. I have your scent now, and I can promise you I won't forget it." The rest of the pack growled and snarled their agreement.

SIMON didn't speak on the ride to his meeting with the Conclave. He thought about Gray and Garon and focused on keeping his magic centered and his anxiety from raging out of control. Master Thomas and the other two mages with him didn't speak either.

When they arrived, Simon looked around in horror. They were at the house where he'd found the cubs. "What are we doing here?"

"The Conclave wanted to verify your story. I gave them the facts as you gave them to me, and they discovered this place." Master Thomas looked at him with disgust. "It's no wonder you're worried. I would be too, if I were you."

"I didn't do anything wrong."

"That is not up to me to decide." The other mages came around to Simon's door and held it open. He stepped out, eyes still on Master Thomas inside the vehicle, and was surprised when his arms were grabbed and held behind his back. The mages snapped something around his wrists, and Simon's magic quieted completely.

"What did you do?" He struggled but quickly realized his arms were trapped behind him.

"Until the tribunal is over, your magic has been nulled. For the protection of the Conclave, of course."

"I am not a threat to them, Thomas. You know that. You know me."

"I thought I did, but clearly I was mistaken." He led the way into the house, with the other mages dragging Simon along behind him.

Inside, three other mages waited for them. Their faces were hidden beneath the hoods of long black cloaks. Simon was forced to his knees in front of them. One of them turned to Thomas and spoke, his voice cold. "We've been waiting."

"My apologies. I found Simon with the wolves and had to retrieve him. I'm afraid his deception is worse than I originally reported."

"What?" Simon looked back and forth between them. "I told you what happened, Master Thomas."

"You lied, Simon, and the members of the Conclave have their proof."

The Conclave members approached Simon and laid their hands on his head. He jerked when he felt their magic inside him and tried to pull away. Crying out in pain, he struggled, but they continued their hold.

After a few moments, they jerked their hands away as well. "He has body magic inside him, as well as lingering soul magic." The members of the Conclave all nodded in agreement, sensing the same thing.

"I can explain," Simon began.

"There is no explanation," one of them replied.

Another added his thoughts to the mix. "You admit that you have this Other magic inside you?"

"Yes, but—"

"But nothing, Apprentice. Did you, or did you not, freely accept the magic of Others into you?"

Simon grimaced. Technically, he had allowed the pack to give him some of their body magic. "Well—"

"Enough. Simon Osbourne, you are guilty of betrayal of the Order of Mages, taking magic of Others into yourself for evil uses. You have risked us all with your foolish endeavor."

"No, that's not what happened. Please, hear me out."

They ignored his pleas. "As such, you are branded Sorcerer, user of black magic, and must be stripped of your power."

Simon started shaking and tried to beg them again to listen. "You don't understand. I'm not a Sorcerer. I have used no black magic. I just saved some cubs who were being attacked."

"Lies," Master Thomas said. "I found him with the wolves, and he is bound in some way to their alpha."

Simon turned to glare at Thomas. "You leave them out of this. You know nothing about what went on. You wouldn't even listen to me, wouldn't help me."

Thomas ignored him and looked beseechingly toward the Conclave members. "I feel as if I have failed in my duties. If you permit, I would see to the punishment myself. It is the least I can do to atone for my mistakes with my apprentice."

They nodded in unison. "You may perform the ritual. It is wise that you accept some responsibility for this and know that you will be sanctioned by the Conclave once this is resolved. However, we recognize that darkness cannot always be detected or avoided. You have handled yourself as well as can be expected for someone of your limited experience."

Thomas bowed before them, and the Conclave members trailed away, leaving the two of them alone. Watching from the window, Thomas made sure they were gone before turning back to Simon. "Well, that went better than I expected."

"What? Thomas, why didn't you help me?"

He laughed and grabbed Simon by the chin, forcing his head back. "Because I was helping myself." He shoved Simon, who toppled over backward onto his bound arms.

Crying out in pain, Simon struggled to roll onto his side.

"I don't understand. Why are you doing this?" Simon's mind finally caught up with everything going on, and his eyes widened in horror. "Wait—you were helping yourself? It was you?"

Thomas smirked as Simon attempted to process the new information. Before he could wrap his brain around all the implications, Thomas raised his hands, and Simon saw a burst of red energy coming his way. He tried to roll over to avoid it, but Thomas was too close, and the spell hit him, his entire body going into spasms as it took hold. He screamed, feeling his arms and legs go numb.

"Your naivety is your greatest weakness."

Simon had no idea what that meant, but he realized he also had an equally great strength within him. Closing his eyes, he concentrated on the link he shared with Gray. The metal around his wrists might be binding his mage abilities, but he still had an alpha wolf and an entire pack at his back. He sent a call for help, forcing as much power as he could into the plea. He could only hope Gray could still hear him.

Thomas pulled Simon to his knees, then lifted him in a fireman's carry. Unable to move, there was nothing Simon could do to stop him.

After carrying Simon outside, Thomas dropped him onto the ground. His arm snapped, unable to take the weight of his entire body landing on it.

Simon screamed again, and Master Thomas kicked him in the side. His body flopped over, his broken arm trapped beneath him. The pain was too much to bear, and Simon blacked out.

22

*G*ray looked around at the concerned faces of his friends and trusted advisors. They all felt very uneasy about the situation, but none of them knew what to do. Gray wanted to go after the Conclave and knew the pack would support him. Cormac said his instincts were telling him the same thing, although he didn't believe the Conclave would harm Simon.

Instincts won, and they prepared to go get Simon and bring him home. Most of the pack wanted to go with them, prepared to fight for one of their own. Gray listened to Cormac's advice and agreed to only take a small group. Liam and Cade would accompany Gray and Cormac on their rescue.

Gray left the elders in charge, instructing Aunt Maggie to contact his father and explain the situation. If things didn't go well, he'd need his father to resume his leadership of the pack. He hugged his son and promised to bring Simon home.

Rocky stopped him on the way out. "Alpha, I'd like to come as well. I think having someone from another pack along might help if things don't go well."

Gray agreed. If things did get ugly with the mages, having another wolf not in their pack along could help in any explanations they had to make to the Pack Council. "Come on. Let's go."

They were on the way when Gray heard Simon scream out to him. He howled, and Liam slowed the car. "No," Gray commanded. "Drive. He's hurt." Liam floored the gas, and they sped through the night, Gray tracing Simon through their link.

Cormac snarled in the backseat. Gray looked over his shoulder and saw that his face was twisted in anger, his fangs fully protruding from his mouth. "Damn it. I should have known better. I should have warned him, protected him."

Gray ignored him, keeping his mind on Simon. He tried to communicate with him but heard nothing in return. The silence terrified him, but he knew Simon was still alive. At the very least, he had that to hold on to.

When they got closer, Gray and Liam both realized where they were headed. "Fuck," Gray yelled. "What the hell is up with this place?"

Cade explained quickly to Cormac where they were as they all leapt out of the vehicle. Cade immediately shifted, as did Liam, and the two wolves raised their noses into the night air.

Gray allowed his wolf some control, partially shifting. He was stronger this way, and he was prepared to do whatever he had to do. Cade began to creep around the side of the house, his sense of smell directing him.

They found Simon pinned to the ground, face-up, his arms stretched out and attached to stakes. One arm was bent at a weird angle, and Gray snarled again. Cormac rushed to Simon and yelled for Gray. He didn't need to—Gray was right behind him.

Blood pooled under Simon's wrists where deep slashes cut into his veins. Cormac ripped the stakes away and threw them aside, freeing Simon's arms while Gray pulled off his shirt and tore it into pieces. They wrapped Simon's wrists, trying to staunch the flow of blood.

Simon cracked open his eyes, and he whimpered in pain as they pressed on his wounded arm. "It's okay, baby. We've got you."

"Gray"—Cormac pulled Gray's attention away from Simon's face —"he's lost too much blood."

Gray listened to Simon's heartbeat, heard it slowing with each beat. "Simon, agree to be my mate. I can save you, sweetheart, but I need a better connection with you."

"No, Gray. He's too far gone. I'll have to turn him." Cormac rested his palm against Simon's face. "I won't lose you."

Simon's gaze drifted to Cormac, then to Gray. He smiled weakly and raised his hand to Gray. "Mate," he whispered, his eyes drifting closed.

Gray spared a quick glance to Cormac, who reluctantly nodded his agreement. The vampire didn't think it would work, but Gray knew his wolf, and it would fight to keep its mate.

His teeth elongated, partially forming a snout. Turning Simon's head to the side, he bit into the tender skin between Simon's neck and shoulder, his mind forming the words that would bind them together.

Liam and Cade both growled behind him, snarling and snapping. Cormac turned, but Gray kept his focus on Simon and saving him. He heard a struggle behind him, heard a whimper of pain from one of his wolves. Finally the mating bond slipped into place, and he pushed every bit of healing magic he could muster into Simon.

As he did, he could feel his pack's energy entwine with his, all of their focus on Simon and healing. He hadn't called out to them, but they joined in anyway. Simon's heartbeat sped up again, enough to assure Gray that he was out of danger.

Gray released his hold on Simon's neck and turned quickly to assess the situation. Cade was down and Liam struggled against some sort of spell that held him in place. Cormac fought with Thomas, who screamed as he threw spell after spell at the vampire.

Cormac went down, and Gray stood up and stepped between the mage and his mate. Thomas raised his arms, ready to throw a spell at Gray. Gray realized he could feel pack magic in the mage. Familiar magic. Magic taken from his son. Gray's wolf took over, and he shifted as he leapt through the air and tackled Thomas. A spell hit him that knocked him to the side. Before Thomas could turn back to Simon, Gray was up again. This time, he used the stolen pack magic against the mage.

He called to it as an alpha to his pack, ordered it to stop. Thomas stopped and shook his head. A red burst shot toward Simon, and Gray jumped in its way, letting it strike him instead. He howled in pain, but before he could do anything else, he heard a scream.

Cormac grabbed Thomas from behind and jerked his head to the side with so much force his neck snapped. It didn't kill him, but it rendered his body useless. Cormac's fangs, on the other hand, finished the job in moments. He sunk his teeth into Thomas's neck and began to drink.

Gray watched, waiting to see if Thomas broke free, even though he knew it was unlikely. Thomas's mouth opened and closed in horror, and after a few more moments, it was done.

Cormac dropped Thomas's body and spat, and blood flew through the air and landed over the grass. Suddenly, there was a huge explosion of magic in the air, knocking both Gray and Cormac off their feet.

The air was filled with light. Blue and green streams flew through the air and straight to Simon. They hit him full force before Gray could even move. Simon arched up, his spine leaving the ground beneath him, and his mouth fell open in a silent scream.

SIMON'S senses slowly began to return to him, but he couldn't focus on any one thing. He felt the ground under his back and wondered for a moment where he was. He knew he was lying on grass, simply because he could feel it tickling his neck. As he began to regain control, his memories started to come back to him. *Gray!*

He tried to force his eyes open, but they refused to cooperate. They felt weighted down and sluggish to respond. Simon could hear the sounds of a fight going on around him. Muffled thuds and grunts of pain filled the air, but they seemed to be coming from a distance. But not. Now they sounded too close. He was so confused.

Finally, his eyelids began to function, and Simon was able to open his eyes a little. When he finally got them to blink a bit, he caught a glimpse of Gray standing over him. He looked ready to attack. There really was a fight going on. Simon could hear it more clearly now. Someone was saying spells. He tried to cry out, to warn them the mages were bad. He still couldn't speak.

His body began to register pain, his arms first, and Simon remembered the agony of feeling his arm break beneath him. His wrists were on fire, the skin stinging and burning. His neck was next. It ached, so Simon turned his head a little, thinking maybe he was lying on it funny. Something stretched and Simon could feel a warm, wet trickle start rolling down before it dripped onto the ground. Oh God, Gray had bitten him. Mated him. He'd agreed to it, and now they were mates. He remembered.

He forced his eyes to open fully just as Gray let out a roar and leapt away, shifting to his wolf in midair, his clothes dropping to the ground. Simon tried to call out to him, to make him come back. He couldn't speak, though. A soft whimper of frustration escaped. Why wasn't his body cooperating with him? Why was he so weak?

Simon struggled to turn his head a little so he could see where Gray had gone, just as Cormac landed on the ground several feet away from him. He wanted to go to him, to help, but Cormac was already stirring and began an unsteady climb to his feet. A howl startled Simon, and he turned his head in time to see Gray go down. Then a scream, oh God, it was so horrible. Simon followed the sound and saw Cormac with his face buried in Thomas's neck. Thomas was hanging limply in his arms, his blood spraying out around Cormac's mouth. It landed against the vampire's bright white shirt in a horrifying burst of color.

Simon wanted to tell him to stop, and opened his mouth to try, when lights began flashing around them. They came straight for him, blue and green swirling together in this dark mist of color. He heard Gray cry out as they hit Simon and enveloped him.

Pain. It was all Simon could recognize. So much pain. He screamed but didn't hear the sound. And then there was nothing.

GRAY shifted back to his human form, his body sluggishly responding to his commands. He ended up mostly crawling. Simon was totally wrapped in the weird light, his body actually beginning to hover off the ground. Gray didn't know what to do, and he just wanted to do whatever it took to get to Simon. Arms came around him, and he turned with a snarl to see Cormac holding him back.

Blood dripped down the vampire's face. Gray snarled and tried to push him away, unsure if the vampire would attack him now that he had fed. He'd heard stories of their bloodlust and wondered if the mage's blood would trigger it. He struggled to get to his feet, to get away from the vampire and back to his mate. More arms grabbed him. Liam and Cade held his other side, keeping him back. He howled his frustration and began to shift. His wolf could get away from them, even if he couldn't as a man.

He felt a push in his mind and shook his head to get rid of it. It came again. Cade's voice. *Alpha, stop. Please. You need to listen.*

Listen? He didn't need to listen. Why didn't they understand? He needed to get to his mate. Simon needed him.

Gray! Stop! Focus! Liam was screaming at him through their link.

Hands on his face. Cormac. He forced Gray's head to turn and meet his eyes. "Alpha, you need to get control of yourself. You can't help Simon with this. But he'll need you."

Gray turned back to Simon. He floated in the air, not moving as the blue and green swirls continued to surround him. Gray tried to speak, but he was so far into his shift that he couldn't. *What's happening?* he asked through the link.

"He wants to know what's going on," Liam said to Cormac.

"I'm not entirely sure," Cormac replied. He kept his gaze locked on Gray's. "I believe that what we're seeing is Simon's magic returning to him."

Gray wanted to ask questions and growled when he couldn't. He forced his mind to calm and shifted back to human form. The partial change had helped, and he felt stronger, more in control. "Explain."

"I can't explain it, really. When Thomas died, magic left him and went straight to Simon. But look at it. It's not dark magic. The colors are life and healing."

Gray looked at his mate, noticed Simon appeared peaceful now. The lights began to fade as they were absorbed into Simon's body. They all sat quietly as Simon lowered to the ground and let out a long sigh.

Cormac released his hold, and Liam and Cade followed his lead. Gray rushed over to Simon and knelt by his side so he could lift his mate up onto his lap. Simon's head rolled limply onto Gray's shoulder, and Gray leaned down to touch their cheeks together. He rubbed his chin over Simon's face, letting the bristly hair from his beard tickle Simon's skin.

Simon felt different in his arms. Gray focused and tried to figure out why. After a moment, he realized it was Simon's scent. He smelled... stronger, somehow.

Cormac knelt on Simon's other side and placed his hand on Simon's head. He closed his eyes and concentrated for a moment before opening them to meet Gray's concerned glance. "He'll be okay."

"Are you sure?"

"Positive," Cormac answered. Cormac lifted one of Simon's arms and held it out for Gray to see. The wrist was completely healed. Not the slightest mark remained of the deep slice Thomas had given him or the sharp angle that had been his broken arm. In a panic, Gray shifted Simon's head so he could see his neck. The mating mark was there, very faint, but it remained. Gray let out a sigh of relief and leaned his forehead down to Simon's.

"Is everyone okay?" Rocky asked from behind him.

Gray checked the others, who were all nodding. He had a minor bellyache where the spell had hit him, but other than that, he felt fine. He lowered Simon to the ground long enough to slip back into his clothes, then gathered Simon close again and climbed to his feet with Simon balanced in his arms. It worried him that Simon hadn't started coming around yet.

Cormac seemed concerned as well. He touched Simon's forehead again and nodded to Gray. "Let's get him out of here. I'll know more once we're away from all the collected magic in the area."

Gray carried Simon to the SUV while Liam and Cormac carried Thomas's body. The evening air cooled the lingering sweat on Gray's skin, and he wondered if Simon would be cold. They normally kept a blanket in the back of their vehicles in case someone needed something to cover up with after shifting.

He asked Cade to get the blanket as he settled in the backseat with Simon cradled in his arms. Cade climbed in the opposite side and helped Gray cover Simon. Cormac and Liam put Thomas's body in the very back, and Cormac climbed in beside it. "Rocky, you can take the front," Gray said.

Rocky looked relieved to not have to sit in the back with the corpse. In fact, Gray had never seen Rocky look so unsettled. He climbed into the passenger seat of the car and leaned his head against the window. If Rocky were a member of the High Moon Pack, he could offer him some support as his alpha. As it was, Rocky had to deal with everything on his own.

Liam drove them back to the compound, and for once, it wasn't at breakneck speed. Fatigue seemed to hover around them, and their spirits were flagging. Gray adjusted Simon in his arms and leaned down to nuzzle their noses together. His mate's presence comforted him, even while he worried.

He didn't know what the future held. What had once been a given was now tossed into the wind. He thought his pack would accept his mate, but he couldn't be sure. Some of them still had some doubts and hesitations about bringing a mage into the pack. They weren't strong enough feelings to reject Simon being around, but his new status might cause some issues.

Added to that, Gray didn't know what the Council would say. As far as he knew, an alpha had never mated a mage before. They had taken the rulebook and thrown it out the window. With a glance over his shoulder at Cormac, Gray considered the triangle of magic Simon had described to him not too long ago. Mind, Body, Soul. All three types of magic were represented in the vehicle, on the way to his home.

A month ago, he hadn't even met anyone from the other two branches. Now his mate was one and was related to the other. It seemed more like a circle to Gray, perhaps one that resembled a noose tightening around his neck.

23

*C*onsciousness returned to Simon in a rush. One moment, peaceful calm surrounded him on all sides, and the next, he startled awake in a panic. It took a minute for him to recognize where he was. Gray's bedroom. He winced against the brightness of the lights and lifted his hand to shield his eyes as he attempted to focus on Gray's dresser, to see if Gray had left his sunglasses lying there the day before.

They were where he remembered. Simon slipped them on before sighing in relief. He could hear footsteps on the stairs—and it sounded like whoever was coming weighed about eight hundred pounds. Simon covered his ears now that his eyes were safely behind tinted lenses, wishing he could lower the volume on the world somehow. The bedroom door began to slowly open. Simon braced himself for a herd of elephants or something equally loud.

Garon's head poked around the corner, and when he saw Simon awake and standing, he squealed and launched himself at Simon. The sound vibrated through his skull like a jackhammer, and Simon dropped to his knees with his hands clutching his head.

"You're okay!" Garon screamed.

"Shh," Simon whispered. "No need to yell."

i

Garon looked puzzled. "I wasn't yelling, Simon. Hey, why are you wearing Dad's sunglasses? It's nighttime."

It didn't seem like it was dark out to Simon. He glanced around and realized the only light was coming from a small lamp on the dresser. It nearly blinded him when he looked directly at it, so he closed his eyes and wondered what the hell was wrong with him.

More pounding footsteps sounded on the stairs, and Simon thought if he'd ever wondered what a herd of elephants sounded like, he was getting a pretty good idea at the moment. Gray rushed into the room, followed by Aunt Maggie and Cormac. "Simon!" Gray shouted.

Simon held up his hand in a plea for quiet. Garon helped him out. "Dad, shh. Simon says we're all screaming, even though we aren't. And he's wearing your sunglasses too. I think he's broken or something."

Simon thought he might be as well. He stood up and put his hand on his head to stop the throbbing. Gray came over to him and leaned their foreheads together. "You okay?"

"I'm not sure. Everything seems very extreme right now. My senses are overloaded or something." He felt a tingle of magic when he finished speaking and realized it was Gray using his alpha abilities to help.

Simon felt the magic inside him respond with a jolt. He jerked away and gasped for breath. "Holy crap."

Gray looked hurt by Simon's rejection, and Simon wanted to go to him, but he was afraid of what would happen if he did. His body seemed to want to take Gray's magic in a way it hadn't before. He leaned over and put his hands on his knees. Someone had changed his clothes, and he now wore a T-shirt and his favorite pajama pants, the bright orange ones covered in bacon that said, "Bacon Makes Everything Better."

Normally he didn't notice the pattern, but this time he winced and had to look away. He didn't know how anyone could stand looking at them and wondered how he'd never noticed how dizzying they were.

Cormac stepped up to Simon's side. "Simon, can you center yourself?"

He forced himself to look up at Cormac as he answered. "I don't know. I'm not very good at it."

"Try."

Simon nodded and concentrated. In a snap, his magic felt more stable, and he opened his eyes in surprise. Everything appeared normal now, not like he was standing outside in the brightest sunlight. "That's better. Weird, that's the fastest I've ever been able to control my magic. Master Tho—" He stopped, remembering the fate of his former mentor.

"Yes," Cormac said, "we do need to talk about that *master* of yours."

Gray moved up next to Simon, and Simon reached out to pull him closer. When his magic didn't latch onto Gray's, Simon grinned and wrapped an arm around Gray's waist. Gray smiled and hugged Simon against him. "I'd sure like to know what happened," Gray said.

"Me too."

"Me three!" Garon laughed. He went back over to Simon, and Simon draped an arm over his shoulders.

"I think there's a lot we need to figure out."

Cormac nodded. "The first of which is how Thomas was able to steal your magic, Simon."

"What? What do you mean? How could he have stolen my magic?"

"I don't know, but I think that's what happened. When he died, the magic he stole from you came back to you in a rush."

Simon concentrated for a moment on the power inside him. He looked around at the others in shock. "I think you're right. I feel, well, normal, but better somehow. Whole. This doesn't make sense."

Gray rubbed his hand along Simon's waist. "And that's not all. Thomas had pack magic inside him as well. It's how I was able to slow him down. I recognized it and called to him as alpha."

"But how?" Simon asked.

Cormac shook his head and paced back and forth. "None of it makes sense."

"Sure it does," Aunt Maggie added. "He stole it. Just like he stole the demon's magic and Simon's magic. He was after all three types, and he got them."

"I'm not sure it's that simple," Cormac said. "He must have been draining Simon's magic for a long time to get that much power from him. And what about the demon? How was he able to exploit an Other?"

She scoffed. "It doesn't always have to be complicated. And we may never find out more, although if I know my nephew, he'll be finding out what he can. We should be thankful you all made it home safely and that Simon is free of that… that…."

"Don't say a bad word, Aunt Maggie."

She scoffed again, but Gray nodded, agreeing with her both her conclusion and the sentiment toward Thomas. Simon had a feeling Gray would discover as much as possible about what had happened. Simon would as well.

Garon looked puzzled. "But how did he get *our* magic when the demon guy took it?"

"He must have stolen it from the demon too," Maggie said.

"You know," Simon added, "the demon did seem to have some mage magic when I first faced him. I remember wondering about it at the time, but I don't know that I ever said anything about it to anyone."

"Someone from the Conclave must be aware of this." Cormac ran his hand across his hair, then turned to Simon. "You've never dealt with them before, have you?"

"No," Simon answered. "But I don't know for sure that it *was* the Conclave. Or the entire Conclave, anyway. They didn't even give me a chance to speak."

"That is unusual. From my experience, the mages tend to gather as much information as they can. For them to act first, disregarding the bigger picture, doesn't fit with my knowledge of their procedures."

"Well, I don't think we're going to figure it all out tonight, at any rate. We're all okay, and that's what's important." Gray hugged Simon closer and Garon squeezed him from the other side. "Tomorrow, we'll begin unraveling all of this and try to get some answers." He looked over at Cormac. "We can count on you for help?"

"Of course. I'll do whatever I can. I still have a few contacts within the Conclave, although it's been years since I've worked with them."

"Anything will help at this point. We have too much to lose to not use every resource we have."

"Agreed."

"On that note," Aunt Maggie said, "I think it's time for us to call it a night. This will all still be here tomorrow."

Everyone cleared out of Gray's bedroom. Aunt Maggie showed Cormac to the guest room while Gray and Simon helped Garon get ready for bed. When the house was finally quiet, Gray and Simon slipped back into the master bedroom and stood looking at each other for several long minutes.

"Any regrets?" Gray asked.

"Just that you guys got hurt."

"Nothing else?"

Simon stepped closer and wrapped his arms over Gray's shoulders. "Nope."

"Me either," Gray whispered as he lowered his lips to Simon's. They tasted each other for a moment before Gray groaned and dragged Simon closer. He drove his tongue into Simon's mouth. Simon answered his demand and opened wider, teasing Gray's mouth with his own.

"Dang, you're good at that," Simon said on a gasp as they broke apart.

"Just at that?" Gray smirked.

Simon chuckled and began stripping off his shirt. "I'm not sure I remember. Maybe you should refresh my memory."

"I'd be happy to, mate."

Simon paused and looked up at him. "Wow. It didn't feel real until right now."

Gray tossed his T-shirt aside and stepped in close. "It's real."

"I don't even know what it means to be a werewolf's mate."

"And I don't know what being mated to a mage is like. Don't worry, Simon. We're in this together. We'll figure it out as we go." He pulled Simon back into his arms with a smile.

Simon looked up at him and let out a small huff of air. "It's crazy how much better I feel when I'm in your arms." He leaned forward so his forehead rested against Gray's cheek.

Gray nuzzled into him, and they stood there holding each other for several minutes. "You okay?"

"Yeah. Just in shock, I think. My head is spinning. But I don't really want to hash it all out right now. Let's just make tonight about us. Besides, isn't this our wedding night or whatever it's called for mates?"

Gray lifted one hand to Simon's cheek and tilted his face up. Simon could see the swells of emotion in Gray's eyes, waves of happiness, desire, and even relief flooding from him. Simon began to understand the depth of their connection, of the commitment they'd made to each other.

As Gray stroked his thumb over the light stubble covering Simon's skin, Simon felt an answering surge of emotion. He leaned in and lightly touched his lips to Gray's, and Gray immediately opened his mouth to deepen the kiss.

Simon reached for the button of Gray's jeans and tugged until it came unfastened, then he pulled at the zipper until it was low enough to allow the denim to slide down Gray's hips. He traced his hands over the elastic of Gray's boxers and around to his ass, then he slipped his fingers beneath the fabric to find Gray's heated skin.

Gray pulled away and kicked his jeans and socks off before grabbing Simon. He walked backward to the bed, and when they were close enough, Simon slid his hands to Gray's chest and gave him a little shove. Gray chuckled as he landed on the bed with a bounce.

Simon slipped down his pajama pants and boxers, then wiggled his hips to get them to fall to the floor. Gray's focus zeroed in on Simon, and he leaned up on his elbows to get a better view.

Feeling bold, Simon struck a pose and attempted a sexy look. "You like what you see?"

"Much better than those hideous pajamas, I can tell you that."

Simon laughed and jumped onto the bed. He straddled Gray and ran his fingers through the hair on Gray's chest. When he reached Gray's nipples, he gave them a little pinch.

Gray gasped and arched his hips up into Simon. When Simon wobbled at the quick maneuver, Gray reached up and grabbed his waist and guided him over his still-covered length. The fabric created a teasing friction through the thin layer of cotton as Gray ground his cock up, adding delicious pressure to the crease of Simon's ass.

Pleasure shot through Simon's body, and he dropped down so his chest covered Gray's. He rubbed against the coarse hair and thrust his dick along Gray's stomach. "Oh God," he whimpered, his body thrumming with sensations.

When he slid down so his ass cradled Gray's cloth-covered erection, he gave a frustrated growl and got off the bed. He reached up and grabbed the edge of Gray's boxers and jerked them down in one swift motion. Gray's breath quickened as Simon rummaged through the nightstand drawer and grabbed the lube before pouncing back into his former position.

When he settled, Gray stroked his hands up Simon's ribs and around his back. He tried to pull him down just enough to kiss, but Simon had other plans. He wiggled his way down until he leaned over Gray's left pec. He closed his warm mouth over the dusky pink nipple and gave it a wet stroke with his tongue. It hardened into a tight bud just as Simon closed his teeth over it and gave a gentle pull.

Gray gasped and sunk his hand into Simon's hair, holding him in place. Simon nibbled at the peak, then pulled back and blew a little burst of breath over it. Gray growled deep in his chest, his cock jerking against Simon's ass. Simon bit his lip at the rumbling sensation and reached over to snag the lube where he'd dropped it on the bed.

He squirted a dollop onto his fingers and reached behind himself. As he traced his fingers over his hole, he met Gray's eyes and rocked his hips. Their cocks slid together, the dampness from little drops of precome slicking the way. When he finally sank a finger in deep, he had to stop, almost pushed over the edge already.

Gray reached behind Simon and traced over his stretched

entrance. Simon slipped another finger in and released a little mewl of pleasure. Gray let him push his two fingers inside before adding one of his own. Simon gasped and cried out, the arm supporting him shaking as his entire body trembled in need.

"Now, Gray." He removed his fingers and grabbed Gray's cock, giving it a quick stroke to coat it with the remaining lube on his hand. When it was sufficiently slicked, Simon guided it to his waiting hole and slowly sank down on it.

Gray's body tightened, the muscles of his chest and stomach becoming more clearly defined as he fought to keep himself still. Simon watched the silent battle, heard Gray's breath as he clenched his jaw and let the bursts of air escape through his nose. A low growl rumbled deep in Gray's chest, the vibrations sending shivers through Simon's balls and up his back. He realized for the first time that this man, his mate, was an alpha and more powerful than Simon had given him credit for. His strength was only magnified by his ability to control his own needs and let Simon take the lead.

The thought humbled Simon, and his respect for Gray grew even deeper. He covered Gray's hands with his own where they rested on his hips and held on. He tried to communicate with his eyes his newfound feelings, but he couldn't even define the emotion.

"You okay?" Gray whispered, his voice showing the strain that remaining motionless caused him.

"More than okay." Simon raised up just a little, feeling the cock inside him sliding back out. When he felt the edge of the mushroom tip at his hole, he pushed down again. This time, Gray helped, thrusting his hips up in time with Simon's descent.

Their bodies slapped together, and Simon leaned forward, his lips searching for Gray's even as he continued the push and pull on his hips. Gray arched his head up to meet him and let Simon control the movement.

Simon rocked on his knees, moving faster and faster until he mewled in frustration. "Harder. Fuck me, Gray."

Gray complied, grabbing Simon's hips and holding them steady. He drove up hard, raising and lowering Simon with each long thrust.

Simon arched his back, throwing his head back as Gray pegged that spot inside him that sent sparks shooting up his spine.

He yelled Gray's name as he came, and Gray leaned up to muffle the sound against his lips. Simon bit down, catching Gray's lip between his teeth as he fought to hold back his screams of pleasure.

Gray's teeth elongated against his mouth, then his muzzle began to form. Simon rose, the sticky, wet heat of his release coating their stomachs, and saw Gray fighting to hold back his own orgasm until Simon finished.

The spot on Simon's neck began to tingle at the sight of those teeth. He remembered the strange pain from when Gray had bitten him earlier and joined them together. He knew, at that moment, what he could do to prove his loyalty to both the man and the animal inside him. He tilted his neck to the side and leaned down as Gray stabbed inside him, once, twice, and then a final time. Gray lunged forward and sank his teeth into the mark he'd already placed on Simon's neck.

Simon cried out, the emotional connection he felt with Gray's teeth buried in him devouring his every thought. A burst of magic filled the air as Gray shot his release into Simon's ass. Simon rode the wave of it, the magic inside him swirling in answer to the bond with his mate. He felt the answer in Gray's magic as their bodies and magics joined completely for the first time. When the furor calmed, Gray released his hold on Simon's neck, and his cock slipped from Simon's body.

God, what he does to me, Simon thought as he collapsed on top of Gray.

About the same as what you do to me, *came Gray's reply.*

Simon's eyes shot open, and he lifted his head to stare at the man beneath him. *I can hear you.*

Amazing. I didn't know if you would. I'm glad you can.

Simon grinned and laid his head back down on Gray's chest, his face burrowing in beneath Gray's chin. *Can you hear everything I think?*

Gray chuckled and ran his hand down Simon's back. *Why? You thinking something you shouldn't?*

Maybe.

Uh-huh. Sure you are. You're thinking about sleeping.

Simon's soft huff of air against Gray's neck was his response.

Come on, babe. Roll over so I can get us cleaned up.

Simon grumbled, but complied and slid off Gray to the side. Gray went into the bathroom and returned a moment later with a warm cloth. He wiped Simon down, laughing when Simon spread his legs a little wider at his touch.

After he tossed the cloth into the dirty clothes hamper, Gray tugged the blankets from underneath Simon and straightened him out on the bed. Simon pretended to be sleeping but chuckled when Gray pushed him onto his stomach and gave his ribs a little tickle.

You can't fool me, he whispered into Simon's mind. He moved over Simon and settled next to him on the bed.

"That's good," Simon answered and rolled onto his back. "We have a lot to work out, don't we?"

"Yep, but it will all wait until tomorrow." Gray pulled on a pair of boxers and tossed Simon his pajama pants. *Just in case Garon comes in.*

Simon wiggled into his pants as Gray climbed into bed. They met in the middle, and Simon rolled into Gray's side. Gray wrapped one arm around Simon's shoulders while using the other to cover the leg Simon draped over his middle.

As Simon drifted to sleep, he focused for a moment on the magic inside him, its ebb and flow calming in a new way. Gray's chest rose and fell with each breath, its rhythm matching that inside him. Another breath and he closed his eyes, his magic finally at peace.

He'd longed for home, for family, and to be a mage. He'd received the gift of all three, and couldn't help the small smile that crept onto his face. No matter what happened next, he could cherish the gifts he'd received. Simon let out a long breath, his magic tingling its reassurances to him as he did, before he slipped away into peaceful slumber with his mate at his side.

COMING SOON

Don't miss Body Magic, the second book in the Triad of Magic series, coming November 12, 2019

A pack is only as strong as its weakest member.

Rocky Harris knows how the system works. He's been on the bottom rung his whole life. But when his alpha consigns him to the High Moon Pack to help them improve security, he finds his beliefs not just challenged but outright assaulted.

Cade Montgomery's confidence took a hit when the pack's cubs were kidnapped on his watch. He's prepared to do anything to protect his family, even if it means working with Rocky. Maybe Cade doesn't trust Rocky, but with the turmoil surrounding pack Alpha Gray's unpopular decision to break tradition and mate with a mage named Simon, Cade knows more threats are coming.

Then someone declares war on shifters and puts the entire pack in danger. Cade and Rocky will need each other's strengths to survive the impending battle—and the power of their growing attraction.

Preorder your copy today!

ABOUT THE AUTHOR

Macy Blake believes in unicorns and fairies, in moonbeams and stardust, and that happily ever after comes in all colors of the rainbow. When she's not busy at the day job, she loses herself in paranormal romance, living vicariously through her favorite sexy fictional heroes. These days you can often find her pounding away at the keyboard, trying to capture the magic of her own worlds.

Visit Macy's website
https://www.macyblake.com/

Join Macy's newsletter
http://bit.ly/MacyBlakeNews

Macy's Moonlighters Facebook Group
http://bit.ly/MacysMoonlighters

f facebook.com/macy.blake.1042
instagram.com/authormacyblake
BB bookbub.com/authors/macy-blake

ALSO BY MACY BLAKE

The Chosen One

Sweet Nothings (prequel)

All or Nothing

Nothing Ventured

Next to Nothing

Nothing Gained

Hellhound Champions

Hell On Earth

Hell To Pay

Give Him Hell

The Triad of Magic

Mind Magic